Sara
D0043122

SPRINGSONG BOOKS

Andrea

Anne

Carrie

Colleen

Cynthia

Gillian

Jenny

Joanna

Kara

Kathy

Leslie

Lisa

Melissa

Michelle

Paige

Sara

Sherri

Tiffany

A10

Sara

Eva Gibson

BETHANY HOUSE PUBLISHERS
MINNEAPOLIS, MINNESOTA 55438

Sara

SpringSong edition published 1996

Published by Bethany House Publishers
A Ministry of Bethany Fellowship, Inc.
11300 Hampshire Avenue South
Minneapolis, Minnesota 55438

Library of Congress Catalog Card Number 84–71717

ISBN 1–55661–735–6

Printed in the United States of America

Dedicated to the men in my life:
My husband, Bud,
My sons,
Mark
Darren
Dow
Alan
Guy

EVA GIBSON is the author of six novels for teens. She is also the author of three non-fiction books and several Bible studies. Her latest is a series of Bible studies for women entitled *Discovering the Heart of God.*

Eva lives in Wilsonville, Oregon, with her husband, Bud. They have six grown children and are now enjoying the addition of grandchildren. She also enjoys backpacking, pressing flowers, and reading.

She and her husband attend the Tualatin Hills Christian Church where Eva works part time as secretary. She also revises curriculum, teaches writing classes, and speaks at various women's retreats and workshops.

1

"You don't have to shake," Sara admonished her trembling hands as she applied mascara to her curling lashes.

But her hands refused to obey. A dab of mascara spotted beneath her artfully shaped brows.

She picked up a tissue and rubbed gently. Suddenly, her door swung open. She jumped, her hand knocking a perfume bottle onto the floor.

Sara's blond eight-year-old sister, Amanda, stood framed against the hall darkness, her big blue eyes blinking in the lamplight.

"Sara," she said uncertainly.

The tissue dropped from Sara's hand. "Mandy," she scolded. She bent to pick up the bottle. "It's after ten-thirty! What are you doing roaming around in the night?"

"I . . . I had a dream. Can I come in? Please?"

Sara started to shake her head, then relented. "All right," she said grudgingly, "for a minute."

But the little girl stood motionless in the doorway. "Why aren't you in your nightshirt, Sara?"

"Because"—Sara tossed her head in sudden defiance—"I just wanted to see what I look like dressed . . . like this. For fun."

She turned to the mirror again, examining her reflection. Sara stared back at herself.

Yet Sara *wasn't* herself, really. The light sprinkling of

freckles over her upturned nose was covered with makeup. The gray depths of her eyes, enhanced with shadow and mascara, shone from her oval-shaped face framed by long brown hair.

But it was her open-necked black silk shirt that made her look again. She usually stayed away from such dark colors.

"I don't like your shirt," Mandy said, flipping her long blond hair. "Black is so depressing."

Sara's hand rose involuntarily, covering the gold cross pendant she'd worn as long as she could remember. "Amanda Rose Faulkner, just because you're my little sister doesn't give you the right to say unkind things about the way I look!"

Mandy's blue eyes dropped. "I'm sorry," she whispered, "you just seemed so strange—not yourself at all. And I—" The little girl abruptly turned and ran from the room.

"Mandy!" Sara cried. "The little terror," she muttered beneath her breath. She grabbed her blue robe, pulling it on over her silk shirt and designer jeans.

Sara found Mandy curled up in bed, her face buried in the pillow, muffling her sobs. Gently, she cradled her sister against the old familiar robe.

"Hey, little sister. It's okay."

But it wasn't.

"Sara, are you going out?" Mandy choked.

Sara bit her lip. "No," she said, but inside, her thoughts clamored. *Liar, liar. You're dating someone your parents would never approve of. And no one knows—except Brad.*

She bent over the little girl. "Listen, Mandy. If you'll stop crying and go right to sleep, I'll give you something. Something special."

Mandy's sobs quieted. She turned her face toward her sister. Something inside Sara softened as she saw Mandy's wet lashes stuck into little tepees.

She smoothed the tangled hair away from Mandy's damp forehead. With sudden decision, she unhooked the gold pendant and slid it around her sister's neck. She kissed her quickly. "Not another word," she said.

Sara hurried back to her own room and glanced at the clock. It was after eleven. For a moment, she hesitated. Wouldn't it be better to just crawl into bed?

She caught a glimpse of her reflection in the mirror. Slim, alive, sixteen—too old to be cooped up forever with a family who didn't understand—roped in with smooth platitudes and a love that corralled her. She only wanted to be free. . . .

Sara caught her breath. Her throat looked naked without her cross catching the familiar lamplight, shimmering gold. She turned away, jerking open her jewelry box drawer.

When she crept down the stairs a few minutes later, a silver butterfly nestled in the cross's place. Her fingers reached up, touching the filigree outline, feeling the pulse of fear throbbing in her throat.

She paused halfway down the stairs. Her parents' room had been built out over the garage at a later date than the rest of the house, separating it from the main part. There was only silence behind the closed door. Sara pulled her jean jacket closer. *Liar, sneak!* her thoughts cried.

She refused to listen. Muting her footsteps, she continued down the stairs, through the hall, and into the basement.

Her fingers groped for the light switch. Lights blazed overhead, bringing into sharp relief the outlines of washer and dryer, the clotheshorse pushed against the wall, shelves of home-canned peaches and preserves, and a crazy assortment of boxes.

Her steps quickened as she passed them and headed for the door that opened into the tunnel connecting the house to the street. For a moment, she fumbled with the key, then pushed the door open and extinguished the light.

The tunnel was dark. Only a subdued light from its opening gave her direction. Her feet stumbled on the rough cement. A breeze from the outside blew toward her, making goosebumps run along her arms.

"Crazy," she whispered, "this isn't freedom. It's foolishness!"

Still she kept on. She could see better now since the moon had risen, mingling its soft light with the harsh streetlights. The overhanging ivy growing around the tunnel opening cast shifting shadows along the walls. So beautiful and yet . . .

At the tunnel's end, she reached out an uncertain hand, parting the ivy tendrils. The street climbed the hill away from her, light and dark mingling into a still-life tapestry.

Across the street, windows gushed harsh light into the summer night. High above, an oak tree waved its branches restlessly.

Her heart pounded in apprehension. *Would he come?* The beams of an approaching car cut through the darkness. Sara swallowed hard. *Was it Brad?*

Disappointment enveloped her as a bulky minivan passed, slowly lumbering up the hill. The ivy dropped from her hand. She leaned back, shoving her shoulders against the unyielding cement wall.

She could feel its roughness through her jean jacket and silk blouse. Her hand crept up, fingering the frail butterfly.

The sound of a motorcycle throbbed in the darkness. Another car sped closer.

Sara leaned forward and poked her head through the tunnel opening. The ivy cascaded around her shoulders and tangled with her brown hair. A green-leaved tendril fell across her eyes. Impatiently, she flicked it aside.

Headlights glinted on the handlebars of the cycle, silhouetting a helmeted rider as an oncoming car swayed around the corner.

Tires screeched. Suddenly, car and cyclist collided. As in a dream, Sara saw the rider thrown in an arc over the car's hood and the car careen against the light post.

She screamed. Darkness descended. For an instant, her body seemed paralyzed with shock. Horror cemented her feet to the tunnel floor.

The car crashed to a stop. She heard the door open, the sound of running footsteps. Then the door slammed shut, the engine roared, and tires screamed their agony.

The car tore away into the night, leaving an empty street. Only a crushed motorcycle reflected the cold moonlight.

Sara leaped forward through the opening, the clinging ivy pulling at her neck and shoulders. Impatiently, she thrust it aside. She must get to the injured motorcyclist!

She raced up the hill, her breath coming in little nervous gasps, fear making her mouth dry. *Was the cyclist dead?* Had the driver who'd struck him down been Brad, her forbidden date?

Horror welled up in her throat. *Oh, God,* her thoughts cried. *Oh, God, please help!*

The cyclist lay beside the road, face down. Sara knelt beside him. A quiet strength she didn't know she possessed rose inside her.

She slid her hand beneath his head, turning it slightly to one side. Her fingers explored his face, hovering before his mouth and nose. Her heart leaped as she felt the warmth of his breath.

She bent lower. "Are you all right?" she whispered.

The man's eyelids fluttered. He licked his lips.

He's young, Sara thought, noting the smooth cheek and the firm chin.

She touched his forehead. "You're not alone," she said.

"My name is Sara. I'll try to stay with you, but somehow we have to get help."

His eyes were open now, watching her. Alarm leaped into them. "No," he whispered, "don't leave me. . . ." His voice lowered even further. Sara thought she heard him add ". . .alone."

Pain wrenched his face, and he rolled clumsily onto his side. "My hand—"

Sara gasped. Blood pulsated from his wrist, staining his fingers. She jerked her jacket off her shoulders and bound it snugly around the injured hand, elevating it.

Someone come quick. Come quick! her thoughts screamed. She looked down at his pale face. His eyes closed in apparent pain. Should she stay? Run for help?

Lights blossomed in the downstairs window of her house. Her chin jerked. Had her parents heard the crash?

A car turned the corner, flooding her in brightness. Frantically she waved her hand. "Stop!" she screamed. "Stop!"

This time the screech of tires comforted her. A heavy-set man hurried toward her.

"Call an ambulance!" she shouted. "He's hurt." She pointed to her house. "There's a phone there."

The man ran back to his car. Sara watched him drive to her house and stop.

Once again she bent over the injured young man. His breath was shallow. Her light jean jacket around his wrist rapidly darkened in the moonlight. "He's gone for help," Sara said. "He'll call an ambulance—get you to a hospital."

The man's eyes opened again. Sara saw a great weariness in their shadowed depths.

"Thanks," he murmured. "You're an angel." Once more his eyelids closed.

Sara's lips trembled. *Oh no, I'm not!* she wanted to cry. *If you only knew!*

Instead she said, "My house is close by. He went there to call for help." *Oh, hurry!* she cried inwardly as she noted the stain widening on her jacket. Aloud she said, "They're coming! My dad's with them!"

"Sara!" her father cried. "Sara?"

"Yes. Come quickly!"

He was beside her in a moment, his hand under hers, relieving her of the weight of the man's arm. "I've called an ambulance," he said.

The young man's eyes opened. "Police?"

Her father nodded. "They'll want to find out what happened. Do you know?"

The heavyset man who had brought her father pushed forward. He was broad-shouldered and dressed in tan coveralls that zipped to the neck. His small eyes, embedded in his beefy face, snapped with excitement.

"Your motorcycle is a total wreck. What hit you?"

The weary eyes opened again, then closed. "I . . . I didn't see. I can't remember. I . . ."

Sara touched his cheek lightly. "Don't worry right now," she pleaded. "Later."

The beefy man's hand smashed down hard on her shoulder. "What about you? Did you see anything?"

A strange iciness settled into Sara's stomach. "I—"

His hand tightened and Sara winced.

"Where were you when it happened, anyway?" the man asked.

"Sara?" Her father seemed to echo the question.

Sara pulled her attention away from the injured man and looked at her father—a tall man with thick, dark eyebrows, casually dressed in blue jeans and an unbuttoned flannel shirt. A questioning frown cloaked his face. She sensed his fear as he probed the tense lines in her face. But she could only shake her head.

The whine of a siren cut through the night, growing louder and louder.

"Sara," her father's low voice entreated. His intense hazel eyes riveted on her.

Sara bit her lip. Was he noticing her carefully made-up face, her silk blouse, her snug jeans?

She felt an unexpected longing for her jean jacket.

A police car and a rescue squad, their red-blue lights flashing, veered simultaneously around the corner. Sara leaned over the injured cyclist and whispered, "They're here. You'll be all right now."

Two men from the emergency vehicle converged around him as she stepped back. An authoritative-looking young policeman took charge as an ambulance rolled to a halt beside the other vehicles.

The policeman's questions and loud explanations from the man in the coveralls blended into confusion. Two attendants appeared with a stretcher and lifted the injured man onto it. Sara had a fleeting last glimpse of his pale face with closed eyes. She buried her head in her father's arm.

She shivered. Tears burned her eyes as her father pulled the soft folds of his flannel shirt around her shoulders.

She looked up. "Dad," she whispered, gesturing toward the crumpled cycle. "It's partly my fault. I . . . I . . ."

The policeman pushed close. "Were you a witness to the accident?" he asked Sara.

Sara's eyes never faltered from her father's. "Yes."

"Your name?"

"Sara Faulkner." Even as she answered, she saw hurt flare in her father's eyes. "I'm sorry, Dad," she blurted. "But I was waiting, hiding in our tunnel, looking out when that car came around the corner and—"

The officer's pen flicked impatiently. "What kind of car was it?"

"Light-colored. I'm not sure."

"License number?"

Sara shook her head.

"Did you see a face? Anything you could identify?"

"No . . . except I think"—her words came out in a rush—"he might be someone named Brad." Sara's agonized eyes sought her father's. "I was going to go out with him and—"

The policeman put his pen down. "Never came, huh?"

"I . . . I don't know. Whoever hit the motorcyclist—"

"Matt Roberts is his name," the officer interrupted. "Go on."

"The driver of the car stopped for a minute, opened the door, and ran over to . . . Matt. Then all of a sudden he rushed back and revved his engine—"

"Took off?"

Sara nodded.

"This Brad," the officer pursued. "What's his last name?"

"I don't know. He never told me. I shouldn't have said I'd meet him, but I did."

"You're not sure if the person who hit Matt was really Brad?"

"No," Sara whispered. "It could have been, but I just don't know."

Carefully, she gave him Brad's description: dark eyes, brown hair, well-built shoulders, his catlike swaggering stride. "He comes over to the drive-through where I work, and we talk sometimes."

"What kind of car?"

"Different ones. Once it was a Pontiac—dark green. Another time he drove a blue convertible. He said he worked at a used-car lot."

"Know where?"

Sara shook her head helplessly. "No, I don't."

The officer wrote down his name and telephone number, then handed it to her. "Thank you, Miss Faulkner. If you think of anything else—"

Sara nodded. "I'll call—really I will."

She and her father watched the officer drive away. The curious heavyset man in coveralls had disappeared in the confusion. A pickup hauled away the damaged motorcycle. The street that had throbbed with action moments earlier was now quiet.

Sara pulled her father's shirt closer around her. Its warmth and softness comforted her, reminding her of his love and care. With that awareness came a sharp pain. Tonight her parents would know all the ugly details. She had failed to live up to their trust. And that wasn't all.

Sara started to reach for the pendant at her neck. Her fingers stopped in midair. She swallowed hard, her stomach curling into a hard, cold ball. "Dad," she whispered. "Oh, Dad."

2

"I thought I was strong!" Sara cried. "I thought I could just flirt and have fun, but it didn't turn out that way—"

She turned to her white-faced mother, sitting immobile on the couch. "I knew Brad wasn't the kind of boy I should date. But I was so tired of . . . of . . . the 'right' guys—the safe ones you approved of."

Sara fell silent. How could she put into words the feelings writhing inside her? Her longing to break into a forbidden world touched with a hint of danger. Yet she fought another longing—to become a daughter her parents would be proud of, to live for the Christ she'd invited into her life when she was in junior high.

"I know I've blown it," she said bravely. "I've failed you and myself, but most of all I've failed God." She looked her father squarely in the eye. "I know that if Brad was the driver of that runaway car, then in a sense I'm responsible for what happened to Matt."

"Just a minute, Sara." Her father sat down heavily beside his wife, a tiny muscle in his cheek twitching involuntarily. Sara saw him reach for her mother's hand, saw hers tremble, tighten, and cling to his.

"We don't know that—not yet," her father continued. "If Brad is the sort of boy I suspect he is, he might not have intended to show up."

A flush rose into Sara's cheeks. She stared at her parents' clasped hands. Her father's hand—big, broad across the back but short-fingered; her mother's—slender, sensitive. Her long-sleeved blue nightgown flared around her small, graceful wrists.

Mrs. Faulkner suddenly stood, releasing her husband's hand. She paced to the piano, nervously leafed through the piled sheet music, then came back to the couch. She ran her fingers along the edge of the coffee table.

When she looked up, her blue eyes reflected her flowing gown. Or were they bluer than usual because of the shadowy circles beneath them and the worry crinkles knitting her forehead?

"Hit-and-run is a serious offense, Sara," she said, smoothing a wisp of her short brown hair into place. "I hate having you involved, even as a witness."

"But I am involved! And I didn't see anyone I could identify," Sara cried, "not really. But I *was* there."

I should have run away or stayed hidden in the ivy tunnel, she thought. *Then no one would have known—ever.*

Her father spoke. "She didn't see anything, Carol. The lights went out. And she did help the injured boy. If she hadn't, who knows?" His heavy dark brows drew together. "I have to admit I was shocked and sick with disappointment when I found her there—all dressed to go out—"

Tiny pinpricks of shame exploded through Sara's body. She leaped to her feet, thrusting her father's shirt onto the nearest chair.

"You don't understand!" she cried. "You don't even *want* to understand!"

She raced from the room, her father's voice following her. "Wait a minute, Sara."

But Sara couldn't wait. She pounded up the steps and into her room, tearing off the silk shirt, wadding it into a ball, and thrusting it into the back of the closet—as far out of sight as she could. Her blue jeans landed in a heap at the foot of her bed.

She grabbed a flowered-print nightshirt and ran down the hall to the bathroom where she scrubbed off every trace of makeup. Moments later, she lay in the darkness of her room, curled in a tight ball in the middle of her bed. Her hands trembled as she clasped her knees close to her chest.

There was a knock on the door. "Sara," her mother called, "may I come in?"

Sara sat up. "Please," she choked, "couldn't it wait until morning?"

A pause. "All right, dear, but remember, we love you very, very much."

The soft sound of her mother's footsteps padded on the stairs. Sara almost went after her, just to feel her mother's arms around her.

Instead, she retreated into the middle of her bed, the silent house brooding around her. Pictures flashed when she closed her eyes. Amanda in the doorway, her long nightgown trailing. . . . Sara reached up to touch the fragile butterfly. It was gone.

She swallowed hard. Funny, the butterfly hadn't seemed important when she'd first put it on. But now it did.

The words her father had spoken as he'd clasped it around her neck on the night of her eighth-grade honor evening flooded through her. "I'm so pleased with your progress, Sara. You're a daughter to be proud of."

Her father was a man of few words. But that only made what he did say more important. Her mind replayed his admission earlier that evening: "I was shocked and sick with disappointment when I found her there."

Sara couldn't sleep. Turning over, she reached for the switch on her bedside lamp. A warm glow filled the room, accentuating her golden stuffed cat crouched on the rainbow-colored pillows in the corner. Her duck collection paraded proudly on the windowsill.

She slid out of bed and prowled around the room, shaking out her jeans, searching among the bottles on her dressing table.

She walked down the hall into the bathroom, her gaze probing the floor. But no silver glint of intricate filigree could be found anywhere on the hall's light tan rug.

After a while she crept into bed. Tomorrow she would retrace her footsteps to the top of the hill.

Impulsively, she grabbed a note pad from her bedside table and quickly sketched a delicate butterfly. Somehow, sketching relaxed her. At last she could sleep.

Sara sat up, clasping her knees, her heart pounding as the flashing lights and screaming sirens of her dream came back to her.

She got out of bed and moved to the window, pushing back the blue-and-yellow curtains. The lights of Portland glowed before her. She knew that a little to the left, hidden by houses and trees, stood Mount St. Helens. Looming straight ahead, covered by darkness, Mount Hood's snowy slopes rose unseen into the skyline. It was the silent sentinal of the City of Roses, her home since she'd started high school two years ago.

Suddenly, Sara wished she could leave the noisy streets behind. There were meadows at Mount Hood, hidden lakes, alpine trails. . . .

But not yet. She needed to make decisions and resolve the torment that had risen within her. Regret mingled with waves of rebellion. Together, they poured through her, scalding her emotions.

She thought of Brad—the way he'd smiled—walked. "How could I have been so gullible?" she whispered. "Do I really want that kind of guy?"

She went back to bed, but a new face wandered through her thoughts. Matt—the smooth thrust of his chin, the weary eyes. She wondered if he was all right.

By morning, Sara's confusion had quieted, but she awakened feeling as though she hadn't slept at all. Her gray eyes were clear, her thoughts brittle and sharp with self-judgment.

She hated to get up and face the new day—Mandy, her parents—then going to work in the late morning, smiling, lifting an eyebrow, writing an order, chatting with the customers.

Slowly, she pushed back her bedspread, pressed her feet into the soft, deep yellow carpet.

Quickly, Sara selected gray corduroys and a pink-and-gray-plaid blouse. She would call the hospital, find out how badly Matt had been hurt, and whether or not he was still there.

After she called, she'd retrace her steps and try to find the missing butterfly pendant.

The woman at the hospital was helpful, immediately transferring her call to the proper nurses' station.

"He's in room 203 and recovering nicely from his surgery," the nurse informed her.

Sara licked her lips. "Surgery?"

"On his hand. Nothing too serious," the nurse assured her. "May I ask who's calling?"

"Just Sara. Can he have visitors?"

The nurse laughed softly. "Not right now. He's sleeping. But this evening he'll welcome you, I'm sure."

Sara thanked the nurse and hung up. She turned. Her mother stood in the doorway watching her. A hesitant, uncertain look veiled her eyes. She started to say something, then stopped.

Regretfully, Sara read the disappointment in her mother's quivering lips. A rush of shame poured over her.

"Matt's all right," she said. "Mom, about last night—"

Her mother nodded wordlessly. Her hand trembled as it covered her mouth.

Sara leaped to her side, her hands on her mother's shoulders. "Mom," she pleaded, "I'm sorry. So sorry—"

She pushed her face into the plush red fabric of her mother's bathrobe and felt her mom's hand gently touch her hair.

"Oh, Sara, Sara," she murmured. "I didn't sleep all night. I kept worrying, wondering—"

Sara's head jerked back. Sudden hardness crept into her voice. "You mean you won't trust me now?" Her voice caught. "Ever?"

"Sara!" her mother cried. "I didn't say that! Don't put words into my mouth that I haven't even thought of!"

"I . . . I'm sorry." Sara looked down, carefully tucking in her blouse. "Did Dad say I'm grounded?"

Her mother turned toward the cupboard over the oven and pulled out a box of cornflakes. "No . . . he didn't. In fact, he was horribly quiet. He seems hurt, Sara. You need to show him . . ."

"I know," Sara said quickly. She blinked. The cheerful red-and-white-checked tablecloth suddenly seemed out of place. So did the morning sunlight pouring over the centerpiece of white Shasta daisies.

Dad's hurt, she thought, envisioning him going to work with bowed shoulders.

Mom's cast-iron skillet clattered against the stove.

"Don't fix anything for me, Mom," Sara mumbled. "I'm not hungry." She hurried out of the kitchen, almost colliding with her little sister.

"Sara!" Mandy cried. "Are you going outside? Can I come, too?" Her blond head tilted beseechingly, and her dimples flashed. "Please?"

Sara swallowed. "I was just going to the top of the hill,"

she said with a wry smile, "on a butterfly hunt. Of course you can come. But ask Mom. She's fixing breakfast."

Mandy disappeared into the kitchen. Sara roamed restlessly around the living room, observing its familiar details: Dad's black leather lounge chair with the newspapers still sprawled on the floor beside it, Mom's old-fashioned piano in the corner, Mandy's paper cutouts strewn over the coffee table, Sara's own lavender sweater carelessly tossed over the back of the couch.

Mandy dashed from the kitchen. "She says okay. She'll wait to cook the eggs."

"You mean just to the top of the hill, don't you, Sara?" Mom called.

"Yes! We'll only be gone a little while." She turned to Mandy. "I lost my silver butterfly and chain," she said as they stepped onto the porch.

"Where?" Mandy asked. "Here?"

"I don't know, silly. Maybe on the sidewalk." She gestured up the hill. "Or in the grass up there."

As they walked, Sara recounted the sights and sounds of the accident and how she happened to see it. She described the crumpled motorcycle and the ambulance. She told her little sister about everything except Brad and the part he may have played in it.

Mandy's reasoning was razor-sharp. "You shouldn't have gone out alone last night. You *were* alone, weren't you?"

"Yes," Sara admitted slowly, "right out here."

Mandy looked thoughtful. "I'm glad you gave me your cross." She pushed the collar of her blue blouse aside. The gold cross shone brightly against her tanned skin. She smiled suddenly. "If you don't find your butterfly, I'll give it back to you."

"Keep your eyes open," Sara reminded. "My butterfly could have fallen in the grass or—"

"Into a crack?" Mandy suggested.

They were silent, their eyes examining the sidewalk and the closely-clipped green grass bordering it. At the scene of the accident, Sara's gaze swept over the tire skid marks and the matted grass where Matt had lain. She shivered as she noted the dark stains on the green.

She turned to the high side of the bank. There, just where the grass gave way to earth, she saw something black partially jammed into the ground. She picked it up, brushing dirt from its side.

"It's someone's camera!" she cried. "Do you suppose. . . ?"

"Suppose what?" Mandy asked.

"That this might belong to Matt? It isn't far from where his motorcycle landed."

"Matt?"

"The boy who was hurt," Sara explained patiently. "He was thrown one way, his bike another."

"And his camera another?"

"Probably. Come on, let's go back."

"But we haven't found your butterfly," Mandy protested.

"I know. Maybe it'll turn up in the house. I'm not through yet."

Mandy nodded and raced down the hill, her pale hair flickering with leaf patterns from the morning sun and shadowing trees.

Slowly, Sara unsnapped the case. "A Minolta," she murmured. "I wonder if Matt is a photography nut."

A surge of unexpected happiness swept through her. She could take the camera to him. She would see him again.

She returned the camera to its case, swung the strap over her shoulder, and hurried down the hill. Instead of joining her mother and sister in the house, she pushed aside the overhanging ivy from the shadowy tunnel entrance, ducked her head, and stepped inside.

There was no delicate butterfly pendant to welcome her, only cold gray cement and gritty dust. How different it was in the bold morning light—ugly, uninviting. She shivered as she saw herself huddling in a tunnel, waiting for a boy she hardly knew.

The ivy stirred into a whisper as she stole down the tunnel, then back again. Remembering the previous night's moonlight, she pushed the leaves aside and looked up the hill.

She gasped and shrank back. A boy in his twenties—tall, lean, and very blond—bent over the tire marks. She watched as he stepped onto the grass. He appeared to be searching for something along the bank and surrounding area.

Sara touched the camera case while her thoughts scuttled frantically. Was the boy merely a curious passerby? Could he be the hit-and-run driver? Or was he a friend of Brad's looking for evidence of Brad's presence last night?

Quickly she memorized the set of his shoulders, the curling fair hair. A shiver ran up her arms as she saw him suddenly stand up straight. His hawklike face looked grim as he surveyed her house with a long, meditative stare. Then he turned, strode up the hill, and disappeared.

Sara pushed through the ivy and raced after him. If he had a car parked around the corner, unseen . . .

An engine started. Tires screamed. She barely discerned a flash of gray through the leaves.

She stopped, her breath coming in short, ragged gasps. Disappointment hurtled through her. No license number, no evidence of who might have knocked Matt down, and no butterfly, either.

She looked down at the camera flopping at her side. At least she had that. She'd take it to Matt when she got off work this evening. Maybe they would have a chance to get better acquainted.

3

The thought hit her almost as hard as a physical blow. *You shouldn't be working here.*

Sara hesitated in the open door of the drive-in, balancing a coffee cup on a serving tray. Sara extended the coffee container through the drive-through window to the man in the green Chevrolet. *That's silly,* she thought.

A pair of intense, dark eyes locked her gaze. "I've got more to order, loveboat," he said in a low, melodious voice that suited his dark hair.

He picked up the sugar packet from the top of the container and ripped it open. "I like my coffee the way I like my women—hot and sweet."

A bright pink stole into Sara's cheeks. She lifted her chin. "I can't take your order now," she said. "You'll have to go through again."

Her cheeks burned as she motioned to Doreen to take her place. As she walked through the kitchen, the cook, Lonnie, a quick-moving young man with blue eyes, sandy hair, and too much beard, grinned at her. "Well, Sara, I'm back at the salt mines."

Sara smiled. "How was your vacation?"

Lonnie's beard bobbed as his big hands efficiently steered his spatula over the long grill. "We went to the beach, down toward the California border. Now that's the life!" His spatula waved in the air. "Sand, seagulls, parties, and pretty girls."

Sara turned away. The rush, the confusion, the casual air of flirtation present at the drive-in were pulling her into deepening waters—waters that frightened her.

Quite suddenly, a half-forgotten memory stirred. Mandy, barely four then, had been running on the beach. Closer and closer to the waves she had run. Then as a lacy wave broke on the sand at her feet, she squealed and raced toward her family.

"That wave's running after me. That wave's chasing me!"

Sara's father scooped little Mandy into his arms. "The ocean is like the world," he told her. "It's out to lure us until we're in over our heads. And then, if we keep going out farther and farther, under we go."

Even as young as Sara was, she remembered her mother's quick protest. "Why, Robert, one has to live in the ocean!"

Sara wished she could recall her father's reply.

Doreen tapped her arm. "Hey, Sara, we have customers to please." Sara lifted her head and followed the other girl outside.

The lunch hour gathered in momentum and Sara returned to help Doreen. She forgot her discomfort with "Hot and Sweet" as she kept alert for a blue convertible or a dark green Pontiac with Brad's dark eyes peering through the windshield.

At the end of her shift, she ran to the back room, removed her apron, and combed her hair. She straightened the collar of her pale blue blouse and touched her throat momentarily, remembering her gold cross, her silver butterfly. Then a quick peek into her purse to be sure the camera was still there, and she was out the door, hurrying to the bus stop.

The bus loomed tall in the street. Just as she stepped aboard she heard a horn honk. She looked across the bus driver's shoulders and caught a glimpse of a dark-haired man smiling up at her. She was sure it was Hot and Sweet, the leering man from the drive-in. She drew a quick, grateful breath.

Dropping her change into the container, Sara moved to the middle of the bus. She found an empty seat and sank into it, thankful to be away from suggestive glances.

Once again she opened her purse and looked at the camera. A surge of unexpected pleasure rose in her. *Matt,* she thought, *there's something about him. . . .*

Caught away in her private thoughts, time flew. It seemed like only a few minutes later that she stepped off the bus and walked toward the long, white hospital building.

A soft breeze blew in from the river, whipping her brown hair around her face. She tried to smooth it into place as she asked the receptionist for directions to room 203.

The woman gave crisp, clear instructions. "Down the hall, turn left, take the elevator to the second floor. You'll see signs." The receptionist turned to help another woman.

Sara almost tiptoed down the quiet hall as she reviewed the "turn left, take the elevator . . ." instructions.

She hesitated in Matt's doorway. Would he recognize her, think it silly she'd come?

He lay looking out the window, his brown hair darker than she remembered. Or was it because of the stark whiteness of the pillow beneath his head?

She cleared her throat nervously and stepped into the room.

Matt turned toward her, a sudden welcoming smile lighting his face. "My angel," he said impishly.

A smile twisted at Sara's lips. "My hero in distress!" she exclaimed. She looked around the room. "How do you like it here?"

Matt's smile folded into a grimace. "Boring." He nodded out the window. "If it weren't for the green trees outside and that pair of arguing crows, I'd have gone totally crazy in one day. Actually," he admitted with a rueful smile, "it hasn't been all bad."

"Visitors?"

Matt nodded. "My folks were here. I get to go home in the morning." He tapped his head with his finger. "The doctor wanted to observe me for a while. He said I might have a mild concussion. I told him I was wearing a helmet—"

"You were thrown pretty hard," Sara explained. "If you hadn't had it on, your brains might have been scrambled for good. What about your hand?"

"Nothing much. Just a lot of blood and a lot of sewing." His voice lowered. "I made a mess of your jean jacket. Mom took it home to wash."

"That's all right." She hesitated a moment. "Do you suppose she could see if there's a butterfly on a chain caught inside? I lost it last night, and I've looked everywhere."

"Special, huh?"

Sara nodded. "Dad gave it to me a long time ago. I guess I didn't realize how much it meant until it was gone."

Matt swung himself into a sitting position, dangling his feet over the edge of the bed. "I'll have her look. Sara—you did say your name was Sara, didn't you?"

"Yes. You remembered!" she replied. "I spell it without an h."

"Sara." He made it sound like music. "Sara. It's like you."

"Like me?"

He grinned. "Someday maybe I'll explain that." His smile faded. "What I really want to know right now is, what happened there on the hill? The police were here. They told me you were the only one who'd seen anything at all."

Sara leaned forward. "I couldn't tell them much," she admitted. "After the driver hit you, he slammed into a streetlight and everything went black."

"That's what they said."

A sudden flush rose into Sara's cheeks. Matt didn't continue his questioning.

"I think I might know the guy who hit you," she volunteered.

A light flashed in Matt's eyes. "Really?" he exclaimed. "How?"

Sara looked down, her gaze intent on the legs of the bed. "I was waiting for someone," she explained, struggling for words. "It was someone I wasn't supposed to be seeing. I think it might have been him, but I don't *know* for sure. I didn't really *know* the person I was waiting for, either." She lifted her head.

Matt's eyebrows arched with a question.

"His name is Brad. I was going to sneak out with him."

Matt's hand reached out and touched hers. "You don't have to tell me, Sara," he said gently.

But I want you to understand! her thoughts cried. "It might be important," she said aloud.

"I agree." He withdrew his hand and banged his heels against the edge of the bed. The rails rattled indignantly. "If I could just get out of this jail—"

"It isn't that bad!"

He laughed. "True. Just the same, I want to get my motorcycle back in working order. And I have a job that's supposed to help send me to college in the fall. If I don't show, they'll probably call someone else."

He turned restlessly. "I'd like to know who hit me. People like that shouldn't be running around. They need to develop responsibility, face up to their actions before they kill someone. That Brad . . ."

Sara flinched.

"I'm sorry," Matt apologized. "I shouldn't have mentioned him again."

Sara bit her lip. "It's all right." She studied Matt's face for a moment. *He's different than most of the boys I know, talking about responsibility, facing up to a person's actions.*

"Matt, I almost forgot." She opened her purse, took out the camera, and placed it in his hands.

An admiring whistle escaped him as he unsnapped the case and lifted the camera out. "It's a beauty! But why—?"

"I found it early this morning. It was only a few feet from where your cycle landed, shoved into the bank. I thought it might be yours."

Matt shook his head. "No, it isn't mine. I wish . . ." He looked up. "I have a similar one at home. A 35mm Canon."

Sara clasped her hands on top of her purse. "I was so sure it would be yours. That's why I came."

"Do you think it might belong to . . . that Brad?"

"Maybe. Or someone could have lost it there before the accident."

"Not likely." Matt examined the camera intently. He turned the camera over, rewound the film, then opened the back. "It has black-and-white film in it. I wonder . . ." He laid it on the sheet and looked up. "I have a darkroom. I'd like to develop this film."

Excitement flooded Sara. "Why, Matt, we might be able to discover the owner of the camera from the pictures!"

"Exactly. If we could get a clue to the identity of that driver—"

Doubt nibbled at Sara. "Shouldn't we turn it in to the police?"

"No, I don't think so. They may not think it's important. After all, it *could* have been lost there earlier. And I'd sure like a stab at solving this myself."

He picked up the case and examined the inside, turning it every direction. "No identification. If it's okay with you, Sara, I'd like to take this film home."

Sara nodded as he removed the film, then handed the camera and case back to her.

"Shall I advertise in the lost and found?" she asked.

He shook his head. "Not yet. We'll see if these pictures show anything." He opened the drawer of his bedside stand and thrust the film inside. "Just keep the camera until I call. I *can* call you, can't I?"

Sara nodded as she pulled a small note pad and pencil from her purse. She wrote her name and phone number and handed it to him.

"Thanks. How about your address?" He grinned. "I need to return your jacket."

"It's only two houses down from where you crashed, on the same side of the street." She reached for the paper. "But just so you'll know for sure . . ." She added her house number and street, then stood up. "I need to go. I have a bus to catch."

"I appreciate your coming," he said. "A lot. And, Sara, I don't think you're terrible because of Brad. I want you to know, I think you're special."

Sara blinked. "Why, Matt, I—"

"Do you go to church, Sara? There's something about you that makes me feel you know the same Lord I do."

Sara swallowed hard. "If you mean Jesus Christ, you're right. At least I want to know Him better. But these last few months . . ." She sat down again.

"Tell me, Sara."

The words spilled out then—the unrest and confusion, her weariness with the dull routine of church and youth group, coupled with her longings for excitement and adventure. She told him about her job at the Burgermill and her feelings of being drawn into a world that had a strange appeal, yet was oddly lacking.

"Then today I felt I shouldn't be working there." She related her childhood memory of the pounding ocean waves chasing her little sister on the beach.

Matt scowled. "Maybe you're not quite ready for your job, Sara. After all, people swim in the ocean—scuba dive, too. But they don't just plunge in without preparation."

"That's it," Sara sighed. "I don't know how to get ready. At church we've sort of fallen into a rut."

"It's hard when everybody's running a different direction with jobs and school activities."

"It isn't that so much. We've just gotten dull. Me especially."

Matt rubbed his hand against the edge of his water glass. "You need to get back to God, Sara. Really get to know who He is."

"But I don't even have a spark."

"Yes, you do. You asked Him into your life, didn't you?" Sara nodded. "I know what you mean, though. I had the same problem. Then our youth pastor mentioned that the only way we can get to know Him, really know Him, is by obeying."

"But I try to obey!" Sara cried. "I really do. I even plan how I'm going to do something His way, and then"—she waved her hands in the air—"I flub it. Instead of kind, gentle words, I say mean, nasty, cutting ones. Or I run off when Dad's lecturing me."

"I think it has something to do with being human, Sara," Matt explained. "Even though we're Christians, we've still got to deal with our will to do what we want, not what God wants."

Sara's forehead knit into a deep frown. She crinkled her nose. "But, Matt, isn't God stronger than me? Can't he make me do what's right?"

"Of course He's stronger. But, Sara, a lot depends on us. Every day we choose activities, make decisions. My mom told me once that our actions depend a lot on the choices we make. Are we going to feed our own desires and wants, or are we going to obey God's voice?"

"What do you mean, 'feed'?"

Matt took a deep breath. "Well . . ." He groped for words. "If I'm mostly reading garbage, like trashy novels, or tabloid magazines, I'm feeding my unhealthy desires. But if I'm being careful to read God's Word and let it really search me, then I'm feeding the new spiritual life I've found in Jesus."

The frown faded from Sara's forehead. "I can understand that. I really can."

Matt rubbed his eyebrow thoughtfully. He put his hand down and took another deep breath. His blue-gray gaze wandered out the window.

He needs to get back outdoors, Sara thought.

"It's hard to explain, Sara. Except that more and more, God is becoming a part of my everyday life." He smiled. "But don't go thinking that all I do is sing hymns and read my Bible. I do other things, too."

"Like riding motorcycles?"

"And camping and backpacking, too." He sighed. "And working."

"Where?" Sara asked.

"I have a student position in the housekeeping department of a mental ward. Walls, furniture, quiet rooms—they all get my faithful scrubbing."

"What's a quiet room?"

"A room where they put really disturbed patients. It keeps them separate from the rest of the ward so they can't hurt themselves or anyone else."

"And I'm complaining about my job!" Sara exclaimed. "Yours must be something else!" She stood up, walked to the window and stared outside.

"What are you thinking about, Sara?"

Warmth colored her cheeks. "This afternoon when I was ordering supplies, I got to thinking about how Joseph ran from Potiphar's wife when she tempted him to sin. Maybe I should quit my job so I'm not constantly running into the wrong kind of guys." She turned to face Matt.

"Have you thought about asking to be transferred to the kitchen?"

"Frying French fries? Lonnie does that." Sara looked out the window again and changed the subject. "Do you live anywhere near where you crashed?"

"No. We're country people. We live tucked in among the trees."

Sara's eyebrows arched playfully. "And what were you doing so far from home last night?" she asked.

"My brother lives in Portland," Matt said. He didn't offer any further explanation, and Sara couldn't think of anything to say. The silence grew between them.

"I really have to go," Sara murmured. Picking up her purse, she impulsively held out her hand. "Thanks," she said with a smile.

Matt squeezed her hand reassuringly. "I'll call you soon," he said.

Somehow, Sara knew he'd keep his word.

The sun still shone through the trees behind Sara's house when she got off the bus. It glimmered on the ivy, touching a gleaming leaf here and there, resting for a moment on a solitary rose poking through the tendrils.

Sara passed the tunnel opening and went up the front steps. Inside, the house was silent.

She climbed the stairs and tossed her purse onto the bed. The open window beckoned, and she stuck her head out.

Her father was working alone in the side yard, hoeing around the roses. He stopped for a moment, his hands clasping the handle, his shoulders bowed.

Regret stabbed Sara. "I've really let him down," she whispered.

She turned and ran down the stairs and out the kitchen door. When her father saw her, a slight smile lighted his serious face.

Sara ran to him and flung her arms around him. Words seemed unnecessary. His strong arms around her shoulders were the only answer she needed. He'd help her know what to do about the waves threatening her.

Later, she would ask his advice about trying a different job. Matt would help, too. For the first time in months, she sensed fresh direction and purpose.

4

Sara lay in bed absorbing the sounds around her. Cars droned on the distant freeway. An airplane motor throbbed overhead.

Vaguely, she wondered what had wakened her. A faint uneasiness stirred within. Her body tensed—listening—waiting—aware of each breath she took.

She heard a faint movement outside. It could be a shrub rubbing against the house, except no breeze ruffled the curtains at the window. Straining to see in the darkness, she observed the faint outline of her dresser. A light reflected in the mirror.

She took a deep breath, and it was almost as if the entire room breathed with her. She sneezed and the illusion shattered. Tossing back the covers, she jumped up and went to the window.

The side yard was bathed in a delicious combination of moonlight and yellow glow from the streetlights. The top of her dad's tool shed glinted silver, and leaves made mysterious patterns on the grass.

A dark shadow directly beneath her moved stealthily, and a rubbing sound drifted upward. Was someone trying to pry open the kitchen window?

Fear clawed at Sara's throat. She stifled a sudden impulse to toss her stuffed cat on top of the shadow creature and utter a horrible cat squall.

Instead she ran out of her room and down the stairs.

"Dad!" she cried, bursting into her parents' room. "Someone's trying to get in the kitchen window!"

The light flashed on. Her father bolted out of bed in one swift motion.

"Sara!" her mother cried, "run upstairs. See if Mandy's okay."

Sara took the steps two at a time. Mandy's room was dark and quiet, the only sound her gentle breathing. Sara backed out and scurried downstairs, almost colliding with her father, who was still in his pajamas.

"No one's there, Sara," he said.

"But I saw something!"

"The light may have frightened off whoever it was. We can be thankful." Dad moved into the kitchen, and Sara followed.

"I wish I'd done it," she mumbled.

"Done what?"

"Thrown my stuffed cat down on his head. I thought about doing it—then making a horrible cat squall."

"Well, I'm glad you didn't," her mother said as she joined them. She sank into a chair at the table, her knee-length crimson duster and long white nightgown floating around her like a variegated camellia blossom. Sara looked down at her own crumpled oversized sleepshirt and grimaced.

"Are you going to call the police?" Mom asked.

"Probably," her father replied. "But first I need to make sure there really was someone out there."

"But—" Sara protested.

"I know, I know. All the same, I need to check it out." Dad yanked open a drawer. "Why is it that the flashlight's never here when I need it? Oh, here it is."

Sara pulled an old work coat from the hall closet. "I'm going with you, Dad," she said as she slid the coat's bulkiness around her.

Her father merely grunted as she followed him outside and around the corner of the house. He shot a beam of light onto the kitchen window.

"Paint on the ledge looks kind of scuffed," he said, "but it's hard to tell."

Sara shoved protruding yew branches aside and looked over his shoulder. Her father flashed the light beam onto his watch face, turning it to gleaming gold.

"It seems that eleven-thirty is prime time for excitement these days," he said dryly. "Sara, are you sure your . . . your boyfriend might not have gotten his nights mixed up?"

Sara gulped and took a startled step backward. "*My* boyfriend!" she spluttered. "Do you still think I care about him? After he . . . he—"

Her father ignored her words as he sent the searching light along the window edges.

"You haven't forgiven me after all, have you?"

Her father half turned toward her. The flashlight beam dropped to the ground below the window. A perfect outline of a foot imprinted the damp earth beneath the water faucet.

Her father bent down, examining it carefully.

Sara crouched beside him, her anger forgotten. "It's too big to be yours," she observed.

"Yes," he agreed. "It's fresh, too." He straightened, slowly playing the light along the edge of the shrubbery. Nothing.

"I'll call the police," he said.

They went back into the house, and her father poked his head into the kitchen. "How about fixing me a cup of your hot, spiced grape juice?"

"There isn't any in the kitchen cupboard," Mom said. Her fingers toyed with the edges of the red placemats. "I'd hate to go down to the basement right now. Did you see anything out there?"

"Just a footprint," her father explained.

"I'll go down and get the juice," Sara volunteered.

"Sara," her mother protested.

But the need for action pulled at her. She hurried downstairs, ignoring her mother's fear.

Instead of intruders and distrusting fathers, I'll think about grapes, she decided.

Everyone told them their grapes were in too shady a spot to produce, but the grapes obviously didn't know that. Every year the vines outdid themselves, and every year her mom filled the kitchen with their warm, tangy aroma.

Something magical happened to them when they were heated inside the juicer. The green juice you'd expect from green grapes transformed into a pale pink. It brought out the beauty of the dark red blackberry jelly and Bing cherries sitting next to it on the shelves.

Sara groped for the light switch. She gasped. The door into the tunnel swung wide, a silent invitation to any intruder.

For a moment Sara's feet refused to move. Then she rushed to the open door. Someone's running footsteps echoed back at her. She peered into the passageway. The ivy at the far end fluttered in a silent plea.

Cautiously, she moved down the tunnel length, muffling her footsteps. At the entrance, she stopped and parted the swinging ivy.

The street slept quietly in the subdued light. No breeze whispered in the leaves. No car lumbered up the hill. Whoever had been skulking around their house had disappeared.

She dropped the ivy from her hand and returned. A bar of welcoming light lay across the open doorway, framing a section of the tunnel floor. Something silver glinted in the pool of golden light.

Sara bent down. "My butterfly!" she exclaimed. "It was here all the time."

But was it? She'd searched every inch of the tunnel in broad daylight. She couldn't have missed it!

"But if it wasn't there then, how did it get here now?" she asked no one in particular.

Had Mandy found it and then accidentally dropped it while she was playing? Sara looped the necklace around her finger, shut the door, and went over to the fruit shelves. She picked up a jar of pink grape juice and carried it upstairs.

Her father frowned at her. "I was about to go after you," he said. "What took you so long?"

Sara set the jar on the table. "The door to the tunnel was wide open," she said. "I went clear to the end to see if anyone was outside."

"Sara!" her mother gasped, "you shouldn't—"

"No one was there." She said nothing about the butterfly and chain looped around her fingers, nor about the echoing footsteps.

The scowl on her father's face deepened. "Did you leave it unlocked last night?" he asked.

"I . . . I don't think so. Wait, maybe I did." Her own forehead creased into a troubled furrow.

"We're going to have to be careful to lock all the doors from now on," her father said. Worry made his voice harsh. "I don't like the idea of intruders lurking around the house."

"Who does?" Mom asked tartly.

Sara picked up the jar of juice and carried it to the kitchen counter. "None of us," she muttered. She opened the jar and poured three cups, added a bit of water to each one, some cloves, and a teaspoon of brown sugar.

She set them inside the microwave and picked up the butterfly necklace she'd laid beside the jar. As she hooked it around her neck, she wondered whose hands had last touched it—Mandy's, or . . . Her own hands froze over the tiny clasp. Could it have been the hit-and-run driver?

It had been hard to leave the warmth of the kitchen. The comfortable food smells had closed around Sara and made her feel safe and confident.

Alone in her room, self-accusation spit icy pellets of doubt into her heart. What kind of guy was Brad, anyway? Someone racing from the law? A burglar creeping into homes? What was her decision to go with him that night going to cost her, her parents, and Matt?

"Brad," she whispered, "who are you beneath that melting grin—those penetrating eyes?"

She caught her stuffed cat's round-eyed, questioning gaze and grimaced. "I almost tossed you out the window onto his head," she confided. "Sorry, old friend."

She got into bed and pulled the blanket over her shoulders to try to quiet her whirling thoughts. It was no use. She turned over onto her back and stared at the ceiling.

Matt would probably be asleep by now. She smiled as she remembered her visit with him that afternoon.

Abruptly, Sara sat up. She knew she needed to talk to her parents about her job, to try to explain how she felt it wasn't a spiritually healthy place for her to be.

In the meantime, she'd think about God and what He wanted to do in her life. She slipped out of bed and knelt down beside her cat on the soft pillows.

"Dear Lord," she whispered, "forgive me for the way I've been living. Help me to know who you are, and who I am. Please, Lord."

After a while, she climbed back into bed. Her thoughts no longer tormented her. A peace that had nothing to do with her circumstances reached out and cradled her close. Just before sleep claimed her, she wondered if this was the peace that passed human understanding—the kind the Bible talked about.

Sara wakened to a morning sun sliding long golden fingers across the room as it sought its own glaring reflection in the dressing-table mirror. She sat up, surprised that she had slept so soundly after the previous night's fear. She smiled, remembering the prayer she had prayed beside her yellow cat.

This morning, he almost seemed to be dozing. A rumpled pillow hid his face as the sunshine nested in his yellow fake fur.

Sara tossed back her covers and went to the closet. *Something pastel and pretty to match the day*, she decided, tossing light blue jeans and a white blouse onto the bed.

She stopped. She had told God that she wanted to know Him.

Matt had said that the best way to know God was through reading His Word. She turned to her bookcase. Her Bible, which she'd received years before as a prize for learning the books of the Bible in Sunday school, peeked out between *Menfreya in the Morning* and *The Art of Still-Life Painting*.

She pulled it out and sat down in her pillow nest, opening the Bible on her lap. "Where should I start reading?" she asked the silent stuffed cat.

Mandy rescued her from indecision. Prancing into the room, she stepped in front of the sun's reflection, making faces at herself in the mirror.

Then she dropped into a heap beside Sara, exclaiming,

"You've found your butterfly! Where was it?"

Sara cocked her head to one side. "You don't know?"

Mandy's blue eyes stared at her. "No," she said. "Why should I?"

"Oh, I just wondered. It was in the tunnel where I'd looked before."

Mandy was distracted by the open Bible. "Oh!" she exclaimed, "are you reading it?"

Sara tossed her head. "I was—until you popped in without even knocking."

"I'm sorry." She laid her head on her sister's shoulder, touching the delicate wings that nestled in the hollow of Sara's throat. "I'm reading mine, too," she confided, "every morning. I started with John 1 and I'm already at the 'don't let your heart be troubled' chapter."

"Which one's that?" Sara asked.

"Fourteen." Mandy jumped up. "I shouldn't have interrupted you. I'm sorry." She dashed across the room. The door closed behind a swirl of ruffled yellow nightgown.

Sara smiled after her. " 'Don't let your heart be troubled' might not be a bad place for me to begin," she murmured.

The words she read were Jesus' own. "Do not let your hearts be troubled. Trust in God, trust also in Me.

"In my Father's house are many rooms; if it were not so, I would have told you. I am going there to prepare a place for you.

"And if I go and prepare a place for you, I will come back and take you to be with me that you also may be where I am."

She stopped. They were beautiful words, haunting words. They told her what God felt about her! He didn't want her to be afraid. And He loved her so much, He wanted to be with her forever!

She brushed sudden tears from her lashes. Once again, Sara bowed her head. Since God loved her, since He cared, she would give her fears and indecision to Him.

5

"Summer jobs aren't that easy to find," Sara's father protested. He leaned forward, nervously drumming his fingers against the arm of the black leather chair. "Where would you begin looking?"

"I don't know," Sara said in a small voice. "Maybe at the downtown stores. I could sell dresses, or candy in one of the department stores."

"What makes you think the problems you're having now wouldn't be repeated somewhere else?"

Sara lowered her gaze. Was he right? Would it be just as bad somewhere else? No, something deep inside told her she was doing the right thing.

"On the other hand, a new start can make a difference," her dad reasoned.

Sara's chin jerked up. "Oh, Dad, I was hoping you'd understand."

Mom sat by the window, filing her nails. She entered the conversation for the first time. "I have an idea. It's probably not what you have in mind, Sara, but I'd like you to consider it."

She toyed with the file, her fingers sliding back and forth along its rough edge. "Since you think the Burgermill is wrong for you, and since jobs are hard to get, I'd like you to consider staying home with Mandy this summer."

Her husband raised a hand in quick protest.

"Wait," she entreated. "For months Lucille has been

asking me to help in her shop this summer. I've always said no because I needed to be here with Mandy." She lowered her voice, "I wish you'd consider it, Robert. It's something I'd love to do."

A vision of Lucille's bridal shop rose into Sara's mind—pastel bridesmaid dresses, ruffled garters with blue ribbons, the big sample books of wedding invitations and napkins. A certain scent pervaded it, too—rose petals and crisp new laces. She could see her mother answering the telephone, taking orders, talking to customers.

"Spring and summer are her busiest times," Mother pursued, "and right now her husband wants to take off for the mountains. She feels torn between him and her business."

Her father's dark brows drew together. "Is it something Sara might do?"

Her mother laid the file down and stood up. "You don't understand, Robert. It's something *I* want to do. And if Sara isn't happy in her job—"

"I see. So that's how the wind blows." He got up and hugged his wife. "Tired of staying home, honey?"

Sara slipped out of the room unnoticed. Her mother's words followed her. "It isn't that. It's just something I'd enjoy. Oh, I don't know. We're such . . . such plodders. And sometimes I long to work with pretty things."

Upstairs in her room, Sara tore a piece of paper from her notebook and began to write. "I'm resigning my position." Her halting fingers drew a picture of a tall French fry. She added stick legs and arms and drew in a sad face, then continued, "My last day will be one week from today."

She slipped the paper underneath the edge of her jewelry box and picked up her hairbrush. Her bus would come soon—too soon.

That afternoon at the Burgermill, Sara and Doreen sat together at a small table in the kitchen, an icy orange drink in front of each of them.

"I think you're nuts!" Doreen exclaimed. "I know this isn't the best job in the world, but it's not the worst, either." She arched dark brows at the younger girl. "I can't imagine you having much fun stuck at home baby-sitting your sister. Ugh! Sounds boring."

Sara sighed. "I know. It's not what I planned," her voice lowered, "but somehow I think it's what God wants."

Doreen tossed her dark hair over her shoulder. "Why, Sara! I didn't know you were religious."

A blaze of pink crawled into Sara's cheeks. "I'm not exactly," she confessed. "But lately my life has been so empty." She gestured toward the drive-through window. "At first it was glamorous—having the boys flirt with me, feeling pretty for the first time in my life. But now—"

She stopped. She didn't want to tell the other girl about the accident by her house, or the doubts it had raised inside her.

Doreen shrugged. "Well, it's your funeral." A horn honked outside and she leaped to her feet.

After Doreen left, Sara sat still. Resigning from her job had been easier than she'd thought.

Before she had left for work her father had taken her aside. "Sara," he said, "I'd like you to resign from your job as soon as possible so you can be home to watch Mandy."

Some idiotic impulse within her made her want to say, "So? What if I've changed my mind?" She didn't.

Her father looked at her intently. For the first time Sara noticed the dark circles beneath his eyes, the nervous movement of his hand on the garden trowel he was holding.

"I didn't realize at first how much your mother needed a change. I want to give her a chance to try her skills."

"I'll put in my resignation today," Sara said.

He nodded. "Thanks."

Now Sara jabbed the bottom of the container with her straw and sighed deeply. A rough hand clasped her shoulder.

She looked up. Lonnie stood smiling down at her.

"Don't look so unhappy, Kitten. Someday it'll be back to the salt mines. In the meantime"—he raised his hands over his head—"your freedom is there to enjoy!"

"Freedom?" Sara spluttered. "I'll have my little sister underfoot every minute."

"So what?" He grinned broadly and lowered his arms. "Just enjoy those hours when you can be free to—oh, talk on the phone, take a nap, bake a pie—just be with your sister." He went back to his French fries and sizzling burgers, whistling good-naturedly.

Sara smiled. In spite of his sly winks and borderline jokes, Lonnie was a good friend. She'd miss him.

The dinner hour began. Sara tossed her cup into the garbage, pinned on her prettiest smile, and joined Doreen at the window.

She spotted Matt in the line of cars and waved. "I was hoping I'd find you here," he said as he came alongside the window. He handed her several bills.

"Just back from break," Sara said. "How's your hand?"

He raised his arm tentatively. "Good as new—almost. Back to the doctor in a week and off with the bandage. Are my burger and Coke ready?"

"Doreen has them."

She started to turn away, but Matt stopped her. "Brad been in?"

Sara shook her head. "What about that roll of film? Have you developed it yet?"

"No. In fact, that's one of the reasons I'm here."

Sara's brows arched curiously. She stood poised, ready

to hurry about her tasks, a trim, efficient figure in blue jeans and a red Burgermill T-shirt.

"I'd like you to be there when I develop it. I've replenished the fixer and everything's set. When could I pick you up? Or do you want to be there?"

"Oh, I'd love to see how you develop pictures. Would day after tomorrow be all right? I have a day off." She started to tell him that after the end of the week she'd have lots of time, but she shut her lips determinedly. Later.

Quickly, they made arrangements for him to come to the house and meet her parents. "They might not let me because . . . because of Brad," she confessed. "But we can at least try."

He nodded in understanding and drove away. After that, there were more Cokes, hot coffee, hamburgers, and a never-ending stream of French fries to serve.

And all the time Sara's heart sang. *He makes me feel good about myself,* she thought, *while Brad, even when I thought he was so special, never did.*

Now when she thought about Brad, she was reminded of Hot and Sweet. They had the same dark eyes, the same suggestive intentness in their depths. Sara shivered. She thrust her thoughts aside and concentrated instead on clearing trays and serving customers.

It was almost time for her shift to end when she looked out the window and saw a green car that looked familiar. Brad—but it wasn't Brad at all. Her lips curled in revulsion as Hot and Sweet smiled at her. Sara stepped back.

"Sorry," she said. "I'm off duty now."

She touched Doreen's shoulder, then marched through the kitchen to the small room where the employees kept their belongings. She picked up her purse and slipped into her dark blue cardigan. Back in the kitchen, she stopped and looked outside.

The green Chevrolet sat in the parking lot. A wave of

unexplained fear swept over her. She sat down abruptly at the table in the kitchen.

"What's the matter, Sara?" Lonnie teased. "Can't you bear to be parted from your job?"

Sara licked her lips nervously. "Not exactly. I'm just hungry, I guess." She smiled mischievously and banged her hand on the table. "How about some service around here? I want a hamburger and lots of French fries. And a milkshake—chocolate."

Lonnie threw up his hands in mock horror, his spatula spattering grease down his apron front. "Coming up, madam. My very best creation. With onion, pickles, tomatoes, and relish."

"Don't forget the catsup and mustard! And how about a slice of cheese, melted to make it yummy."

"Girl, why don't you ask for a cheeseburger?" Lonnie slapped a hamburger onto the grill. "But the customer is always right. When you ask for service, you get it. I hope you can pay for this thing."

Sara laughed. "But, sir, it's on the house! My going away present, if you please."

By the time Lonnie served her, they were both giggling. Sara made a point of lingering over her meal. She didn't slip out the back until she was sure Hot and Sweet was long gone.

She arrived home later than usual. Even before she stepped onto the porch, she heard the musical strains of her mother's favorite piano concerto. Sara smiled. *Mom's happy,* she thought.

Mandy whirled from couch, to window, to chair, improvising her own dance steps. She danced toward her sister without missing a beat and threw her arms around her.

"Mom's going to be working at the bridal shop," she cried. "I get to be your girl!"

Her mother stopped playing and swung around on the

piano bench. "It's true," she said with a smile. "I start next week."

"I'm glad," Sara replied.

"There's chicken and a baked potato in the microwave," Mom said.

"Oh, I should have called," Sara apologized. "I ate at work."

She wandered into the kitchen anyway. A glass of milk would taste good. Mandy followed her. She gyrated around the counter which jutted into the room. Then she spun in an odd pirouette, right in the center of the kitchen, banging her foot into a cabinet.

"Careful, Mandy," Sara cautioned. She offered Mandy a glass of milk and they sat down together on the counter stools.

"I get to be your girl. I get to be your girl," Mandy chanted.

"Hush," Sara admonished. "You'll make Mom feel bad."

A pained expression crossed Mandy's face. "Oh," she said. "I didn't think—" Her mouth twisted in consternation. She jumped up and raced into the living room, leaving her milk behind.

"She's a tender little kid," Sara mused. She finished her own milk, told her mother and sister good-night, and went upstairs. The evening was young, but she felt suddenly weary. She folded back the bedspread and began to undress.

After crawling into bed, she opened her Bible. She only read a few verses from John 14. "Peace I leave with you; my peace I give you. I do not give to you as the world gives. Do not let your hearts be troubled and do not be afraid."

She turned out the light. The darkness closed around her, heavy and oppressing. She got up and went to the window, releasing the shade and opening the window wide. The air swept in, warm and sweet, full of flower scent and the tang of bruised sage. She smiled. *Dad and his green thumb.*

She lay awake a long time listening to a pair of frogs from the neighbor's pond croaking to each other.

Suddenly, the sound of hurrying footsteps wakened her. For a moment she couldn't put it together. How long had she been asleep? Was someone still up?

She turned onto her side. The red numbers on her clock radio shone 3:47. The frog voices were silent.

Her father's distinct, deep voice drifted up to her room, although his words were unintelligible. It didn't come from her parents' room either. Quite obviously, her parents were moving around. But why?

Sara jumped out of bed and reached for her robe. Its long blue folds settled around her. She sped down the stairs.

Mom stood in the open doorway of the living room, unbelief painted on her pale, strained face. She gestured wordlessly toward the dining room.

Sara brushed past her. Her father looked up from the telephone, a frenzied expression in his eyes. "Police? Yes. We've just been burglarized. I think someone came in through the window."

Sara followed the direction of his look and ran toward it. She pushed the drapes aside and leaned far out into the night.

"Sara!" her mother cried. "Get back!"

Sara scarcely heard her. An unseen car motor throbbed. Then the sound faded, swallowed up in the distant noise of the freeway.

She pulled her head inside and turned to her mother. "Was anything taken?"

"The small stereo in the dining room." Mom's voice wavered. "The drawers in the buffet were left open, too. We haven't been able to determine if anything else is gone."

Sara ran into the dining room and stopped short. The

havoc was incredible: drawers were crazily askew, papers drifted onto the floor.

"How could we have slept through this!" Sara cried. She flew into the kitchen. Even there, drawers and cabinets remained open.

"Great-grandmother's vase!" Mom cried. "It's gone!"

Sara looked at the windowsill where the antique vase had long stood catching the sun's rays, turning the cut glass a mysterious violet flushed with pink.

"Don't touch anything," her father warned. He put his arm around her mom. "I'm sorry about your vase, honey. I wish . . ."

They wandered through the house. "I just don't understand," Mother kept repeating. "It isn't right."

While her parents were preoccupied, Sara slipped downstairs. Her fingers trembled as she turned on the basement light, but the tunnel door was securely locked. She tiptoed across the cement floor. The key wobbled as Sara placed it in the lock, and she wondered what she expected to find—more running footsteps, someone lurking in the shadows?

She pushed the door open and peered down the tunnel into the empty street. The air seemed oppressive, and even the ivy failed to wave a tendril. The waiting hush of approaching dawn pressed around her.

A car stopped by the entrance and Sara moved forward. Lights illumined the interior of a police car. Sara swallowed hard as she recognized the officer who had questioned her the night of Matt's accident.

"I should tell him about those running footsteps the other night—and the camera," she whispered. "They might think it's important, even though Matt said they probably wouldn't."

Quite suddenly the frog pair resumed their croaking.

Sara breathed a prayer. “Come here, Lord,” she murmured, “right now. I need you.”

She turned and went back inside.

6

Sara's entrance couldn't have been better planned if she'd stood outside the basement door and waited for a cue.

The broad-shouldered policeman and her parents looked up as she came into the kitchen. The policeman nodded his head in greeting. "I was just asking your folks if you'd seen anything of Brad, or picked up any information."

Sara licked her lips. "You mean about the accident?"

Officer Peterson leaned forward, his blue eyes flashing concern.

She took a deep breath. "Are you connecting that with this—?" She gestured around the the disheveled room.

"Are *you*?" he asked.

"I . . . I'm beginning to wonder—" She looked at her father, an unspoken appeal in her eye. "Dad . . ."

Dad reached for her mother's arm. "Let's leave Sara alone to talk to the officer." He turned to the policeman. "If you have any more questions . . ."

The policeman stuck out his hand. "We'll be in touch."

Sara saw her parents exchange a look as they left the room. Officer Peterson smiled at her and pulled out a chair.

Sara sat down feeling awkward. She'd changed into jeans and a polo. Her fingers went to her collar, nervously creasing and uncreasing its edges.

Her words came out in a rush. She told him all about the camera she'd found at the accident scene, the blond fellow who, after apparently looking for something, had stopped and stared at their house with a menacing gaze. She also mentioned Brad's recent absence from the Burgermill, although he'd been frequenting it for weeks.

"Did you ask the customers he used to hang around with if they'd seen him?"

Sara shook her head. "He wasn't that sort of person. In a way he was a loner. I don't think I ever saw him with anyone."

Officer Peterson slung himself into the chair facing her, his square forehead wrinkling in concentration. "Anything else?"

"Just that the other night—when we heard the prowler—I went downstairs. The door to the tunnel was wide open, and I heard running footsteps. I didn't see anything—except this." Her fingers slid beneath the silver butterfly at her throat. "I lost it the night of Matt's accident."

"Could you have dropped it before you went up the hill?"

"No, I searched everywhere, and so did my little sister. It wasn't there when we retraced my footsteps."

Officer Peterson put his chin into his cupped hand, hunching his shoulders forward. "Sara," he said, "in some ways it hangs together, and in others it doesn't. About the camera—"

"The camera's upstairs in my room, but I gave the film to Matt when he was in the hospital. We thought we might find a clue if we developed it."

"And have you?"

"Developed the film? Not yet. We're planning to tomorrow."

Officer Peterson's fingers drummed restlessly on the table. "Make two copies, will you? I want to see those photos myself." He stood. "I appreciate your cooperation, Sara. And listen, don't lie awake nights worrying about that burglar. We'll keep a close watch on you."

A warm glow swept over her. "I won't," she said. "And I'll have the pictures for you tomorrow—no, wait. Matt said they'd have to dry overnight."

Officer Peterson nodded. "Day after tomorrow. I'll come by."

They walked to the door. The policeman hesitated an instant before opening it. "Sara," he said, "don't be afraid to confide in your parents. They're good people." His hand raised in a quick farewell, then he was gone.

Carefully, Sara locked the door. She went back upstairs but not to sleep. Her thoughts whirled helplessly, sucking her into a well of weary confusion.

That night the dream came again. It was a dream she had had many times before, as far back as she could remember. Sometimes variations colored the details, but it was always basically the same.

Something dreadful happened in her dream, and Sara was never quite sure what it was. But she knew she must telephone for help.

Her heart would pound furiously and her hands tremble as she dialed. And then a voice: "I'm sorry. Your call cannot be completed as dialed. Please check the number and dial again, or ask your operator for assistance."

She would slam down the receiver, lift it, and dial again. Nothing—no tone—nothing.

She would try again. This time, a busy signal.

Sara wakened. Her heart thudded. It had only been a dream. But this time something unusual nibbled at her consciousness. She frowned, trying to grab hold of the difference, wondering why it seemed so important.

Mandy—she'd been alone with Mandy. And something horrible had happened. . . .

Sara jumped out of bed and hurried to her sister's room. Mandy slept peacefully, her arms circled over her head, one bare foot sticking out from the bedding.

Sara pulled the blanket over the protruding foot, and Mandy stirred. "Mamma," she murmured. A sleepy smile slid across her face, and she turned onto her side.

Sara bent and lightly kissed her cheek. She returned to her room, curiously peaceful. The sight of her little sister had banished the dream. She could sleep now.

Morning light spangled the breakfast table with gold squares and dazzled a fistful of dandelions that Mandy had shoved into a miniature vase.

Sara's father sat alone, hunched over a steaming cup of black coffee. The lines in his brow deepened as she seated herself opposite him. "Sara," he said, "I don't want you to quit your job at the Burgermill."

Sara started to open her lips, but he silenced her with a sweeping gesture. "That havoc last night—I can't have two girls staying alone—even in daylight."

Sara glanced around the room. "How did you get it straightened up so quickly?"

Dad rubbed the dark stubble on his chin. "Your mother and I worked for quite a while after you went upstairs. And, Sara, I'd rather you said nothing to Mandy. I'd hate to frighten her."

Sara nodded. "But she'll wonder, Dad. She was all excited yesterday when she told me about Mom's job and my staying with her."

Her father sighed. "I know. She'll just have to attribute it to the peculiarities of adults. I'm sorry, honey."

"It's all right," Sara replied. She picked up a neatly folded cloth napkin and fingered the edges. "Dad, would it seem right to you if I left my job anyway, even if I wasn't needed to help with Mandy?"

"We talked about that earlier, Sara. Jobs aren't that plentiful now."

"I know. But if I just stay home—"

"What would you do with your time, Sara? Most of your friends are away or working. Idleness can be just as harmful as working in the wrong job."

"I could learn a craft. Your grandmother made samplers. Maybe I could, too. Besides, Dad, I'm a little bit afraid."

Her troubled gray eyes met his steady ones. "I can't help but feel there's some connection between Brad, the hit-and-run driver, and the intruder we had last night." She gestured around the room.

"Did you tell the police?"

Sara nodded. "He said he'd keep an eye on the house. But he can't watch the drive-in or follow my bus around."

"Are you sure you're not magnifying things? Putting together the wrong pieces?"

"I don't know." She stared down at the table, then changed the subject abruptly. "I went to see Matt when he was in the hospital. He came over to the Burgermill last night."

"And?" her father probed.

"He asked if he could take me out to his house tomorrow and show me his dark room." Quickly she told him about the camera she'd found the morning after the accident. "Officer Peterson agrees we might find a clue in the film. Matt and I would like to develop the roll together."

Mr. Faulkner sighed deeply. "What kind of boy is he, Sara? He looked like a nice person, but—"

"I don't know him very well," Sara confessed. "But he seems all right. We even talked about God."

Her father's fingers traced around the top of his coffee cup. "Sara, I appreciate your asking me about this. When I found out about your interest in Brad, I was disappointed and angry. Deep inside I felt we'd failed each other. I even determined it would be a long time before I'd let you date again—even boys from church."

He reached out and touched her hand. "I know you've felt that I've been watching you—and I have. Once someone lets me down, I have a hard time trusting that person again. I keep waiting for proof that it's okay to trust. But, Sara, I've noticed a change in your attitude. It's been good."

A warmth slid into the corners of Sara's heart, banishing the dark shadows lurking there. The silence trembled between them.

"It isn't really a date," she said after a while. "In fact, if you said that to Matt, I think it would scare him to death!"

She pursued the subject thoughtfully. "I get the impression that girls don't mean much to him aside from friends. He's all wrapped up in wanting to know who God is, and birds—"

"And motorcycles and film developing?"

Sara grinned. "You said it!"

Her father stood up abruptly. "Go ahead, Sara," he said with quick decision. "Maybe it's an answer to prayer."

He strode out of the room, and Sara sat still, her mood spiraling to meet the gold dandelions, the warm sunshine. Her dad was starting to trust her again. That, too, was an answer to prayer.

Quite suddenly, Sara bowed her head. "Lord," she whispered, "if you want me to keep working at the Burgermill, you'll have to give me strength. But, Lord, it does seem like Mom needs a change right now. Would you show Dad that Mandy and I will be safe together here alone?"

The answer to Sara's prayer came from a totally unexpected source. Her shift at the Burgermill had been busy and uneventful—no sign of Brad, nor Hot and Sweet. Even

Doreen and Lonnie were quieter than usual.

Back home, when Sara stepped onto the porch, a movement in the window caught her eye. A huge brown dog looked out at her, its mouth wide and opened in a distinct smile framing big, white teeth.

The front door burst open and a very animated Mandy dashed through it.

"It's Boris!" Mandy cried. "He's a dog, and he's come to live with us to be our protector!"

The head vanished from the window and reappeared at Mandy's shoulder. "Why, he's as big as a . . . a pony!" Sara gasped. "Whatever will we do with him?"

The dark hulk advanced toward her, his long tail wagging. "I've never seen such a huge dog. What kind is it anyway? Where did he come from?"

"He's a Great Dane! And would you believe it? He weighs one hundred seventy-five pounds! Dad and I went across town after he got off work and brought him home in the car."

Mandy giggled. "He sure looks funny. Daddy wanted to call him Samuel, but the man who owned him said, 'Please, call him Boris.' "

"Samuel? Why Samuel?"

"Because it means 'asked of the Lord.' Daddy had asked God for him, you see . . ." She raised her eyebrows, twisting her mouth into a rosebud. "He told me about the burglar last night. He said he wasn't going to at first, then changed his mind."

Sara nodded. She looked at the dog thoughtfully. "He's such a huge beast he could easily handle three names. How about Samuel Boris Faulkner?"

Mandy looked doubtful. "Sam doesn't suit him. And the man who raised him asked us to call him Boris."

Mom joined them on the porch. Sara looked at her closely. Last night's upheaval didn't seem to have affected her spirit. Her soft brown hair was smoothed to perfection, and her eyes shone with blue lights.

"He certainly is big, isn't he!" She appeared to be trying to get used to the idea.

"What does he eat?" Sara asked.

"Just dog food," Mandy replied.

Sara reached out a tentative hand. "I wish I were a little bit smaller," she said. "I could hop on his back and ride. Why is he wearing a studded collar?" She touched it curiously, fascinated by the bristling stainless-steel spikes. Her hand moved upward. The dog's forehead was smooth beneath her exploring fingertips.

"He's very gentle," Mom said. "The collar helps make him seem more . . . more formidable to intruders." She turned to Mandy. "Run inside and get a handful of dog food, honey. He's cute when he eats."

Mandy hurried out, and her mother spoke softly to Sara. "He's an answer to prayer," she confided. "This morning your father said, 'No way am I going to let Sara stay home alone with Mandy, even in daylight. Not with the problems we've been having.' " She ran her hand over Boris's back. "And then at work he saw an ad on the bulletin board. It just hit him all at once—a great big watch dog. And with me in the position of wanting to say yes for the first time in my life about a dog—well, he jumped at the chance."

Sara's gray eyes softened. "He *is* an answer to prayer," she mused, "for both of us." *But what an ugly one,* she thought.

Mandy ran out onto the porch. She held out a food-filled palm to the dog, and Sara watched with awe as the huge jaws crunched the hard biscuits with ease.

"I'd like a picture of that," she told her mother.

"Why not?" Mom asked. She vanished into the house.

Boris crunched in the silence. Mandy started to give him another biscuit, but Sara stopped her.

"Mom's getting the camera," she said. "We want a picture of you feeding him."

A sudden cry caused both girls to race to the kitchen. Mom stood in front of an open drawer.

"My camera!" she cried. "It was there in the drawer with my film. They're both gone. Gone!"

She wrung her hands. "They even stole the roll I'd already taken." She stared at the startled girls. "I don't understand it. I just don't understand!"

7

"I'm sure now. The camera we found must have belonged to the man who knocked you down," Sara told Matt, concluding her narration of the preceding day's events. "Otherwise, why would he break in and take Mom's camera?" She waited for his reaction.

Matt nodded thoughtfully. The fingers of his unbandaged hand tightened on the steering wheel.

"It sure sounds like it," he agreed. "We'll soon find out. Whoever took those pictures must know there's something there that will identify him."

Sara sighed and leaned back in the seat. A curious calm spread through her. *God must be helping me*, she thought, *otherwise I'd be falling apart, piece by piece.*

She glanced at Matt. A slight frown wrinkled his forehead. Then he turned to her, his quick smile contrasting white, even teeth and a tanned face.

"Everything's ready to go at home, but I need your help." He inclined his head toward his damaged hand. "I can't get the roll into the container without using both hands. You'll have to do it."

"If I can," Sara said doubtfully.

"You'll be able to do it easily. I'll show you how. You can practice on an old roll first." Matt paused. "Sara, about your job—how's it going? Did you decide to look for another?"

"Not exactly. I've already talked to my parents. We've

decided to do something different."

"Different?" Matt prodded.

"Mom wants me to stay home this summer and watch Mandy. At first I wasn't particularly thrilled"—sudden animation tinged her voice—"but now I'm getting excited. I mean, well—I guess it's because I really think it's what God wants." Her long lashes whisked up. "Matt, do you think I'm on the right track?"

"About your staying home or about clues on the film?"

"Both."

Matt grinned. "You're on the right track, Sara—on both counts." He drove the car into a long driveway. "Well, Sara, this is my home."

Sara looked around eagerly. Tall, young firs still tasseled in spring green fringed the roadway. Just ahead, a brown house snuggled into a patch of green lawn bordered with stately purple foxgloves and yellow irises. A narrow cement path guided them into a small clematis-draped porch.

"It's beautiful, Matt!" Sara exclaimed. "Someone in your family must have a green thumb."

"Mom does," he announced proudly. "All spring long she digs in her flower beds, shapes the bushes—"

A woman with a sweet smile opened the door. She had soft, brown hair, and wore a plaid blouse and jeans. Immediately, Sara felt at home.

"Sara," Matt's mother said, "I'm so glad you've come."

"I'm happy to be here," Sara responded.

Matt started to show her the darkroom, but his mother delayed them. "First, come and have some milk and cookies," she suggested. "They're fresh from the oven and oh, so good."

Matt didn't need urging. He poured three glasses of milk, and they all sat down around the table, munching cookies, laughing, and chatting.

Mrs. Roberts was full of questions. What school did

Sara go to? Had she ever lived in the country? Did her church have a good youth program?

Sara enjoyed the conversation and the company, but she was eager to see that film.

When the cookies were gone, Matt and Sara went to the darkroom. Golden cream wallpaper with an eagle design attested that this once had been a small bedroom. Little other evidence remained. A counter with a small sink lined the far wall. In the middle of the room stood a large table, cluttered with film paraphernalia.

But Sara's eyes were drawn to the bold, black-and-white photos that decorated one wall. She stepped toward them. A small dragonfly rested on a large leaf. A bumble bee hovered above a foxglove; water skippers poised on the surface of a creek. Sara almost felt a breeze touch her cheek, almost saw the water quicken and flow beneath the skippers' darting feet.

Matt's shoulder moved close to her own. "Do you like them?"

"Love them! Makes me wish I could—"

"You can." He picked up a roll of undeveloped black-and-white film and pressed it into her hand. "When we get back to your house remind me, and I'll show you how to load our lost-and-found camera."

Sara slipped the film into her pocket. "You must enjoy photographing small things," she observed.

"Sometimes." He took her hand and pulled her toward another display on the opposite wall. Sara caught a quick breath. The enlarged color photographs drew her like a magnet: a sunset in shades of gold and peach above a quiet bay, mallards outlined against towering thunderheads, a canoe reflected in a stream with a lone duck poised on the prow.

"These are my experiments with color. But I don't develop it yet. Too expensive. As you can see," he explained, "wildlife is my thing. I'm happiest when I'm hiking, camping, living off the land—"

"And learning about God," Sara interrupted.

He nodded. "Yes, I have to admit I feel cheated if I can't get up early in the morning and have my quiet time in the woods." He pointed to a photo of a moss-covered stump.

"That's where I go," he confided. "It's so beautiful. A stream runs below. That's where I photographed those water skippers there."

"What do you do if it rains?"

"Well," he confessed, "I just pull my blankets up higher under my chin and roll over." He shook his head. "Not really—only sometimes. Most of the time I get up and open my window and my Bible."

He turned to the table covered with a disorderly array of developing tanks, thermometers, and empty film cartridges. He picked up one of them and handed it to her.

"Just take this"—he gave her a roll of old film—"and thread it in like so."

Sara's fingers fumbled. "You mean I have to do this in the dark?"

"Just do it several times. You'll catch on," Matt assured her.

Sara gained confidence as she threaded and rethreaded the film. Matt handed her the other film and turned out the light.

Sara felt a moment of apprehension. "What if I ruin it?"

"You won't. Just do like I said."

Sara's fingers steadied. The film slid into the reel, and she tightened the lid. "I did it!" she exclaimed.

Matt turned on the light and grinned at her. "Nothing to it," he said. "All I have to do is develop it, then hang the negatives up to dry."

Sara stood beside him in front of the sink, her anticipation mounting. Matt explained each step as he worked. Her fascination increased as she watched Matt agitate the chemicals with a watchful eye on the clock.

But when Sara clipped the negative strips up to dry, disappointment surged through her. "There aren't any faces here at all, just cars. All kinds of them."

They peered at the negatives together, Matt's face reflecting Sara's own discouragement. "Maybe when they're printed, we'll be able to pick up a license-plate number," he muttered.

Sara squinted, tiny lines crinkling around her steady gray eyes. "Matt," she said, "there's one here of a house, an unusual house."

Matt's eyes followed her pointing finger. "You're right," he said. "It looks as if it was built around the turn of the century, like the ones you see in the older sections of Portland."

"Portland is so big," she said doubtfully. "I wonder what our chances are of finding it."

She peered again at the wet negatives. Something niggled at the back of her mind, but she couldn't figure it out. Was it the house? Had she seen it before? Or was it something about the cars?

Matt picked up a lamp and shone it directly on the strips, searching for details. "I wish I had a negative dryer," he said suddenly. "We could print these up in just a few hours." He moved the lamp back to its former position. "We'll have to wait until morning, Sara. I'll do them up first thing and bring them to you. I hope—" His voice dwindled into silence as he took her arm and steered her out the door and back to the kitchen.

Matt's mother waited eagerly in front of the stove, a spatula in her hand. "Nothing," Matt said. "Just cars, cars, cars—all different."

"And one picture of a house," Sara interjected. "But no

faces. I was hoping we'd have something special to show that policeman."

"Ah, well," Mrs. Roberts soothed, "you tried. Oh, Sara, before I forget, I have your jean jacket. Let me get it for you." She disappeared only to return quickly with a clean reminder of the night of the accident. "I soaked it in cold water and the bloodstains came right out," she said proudly.

"Thank you," Sara replied, draping the jacket over her arm. "I almost forgot about it myself. Wait a minute," she said suddenly. "That one car—Matt, could I have another look?"

They hurried back to the drying negatives. Sara examined them carefully. "Look at the third one down," she urged, "it looks familiar."

Matt seemed unimpressed. "Working where you work, they could *all* look familiar."

Sara didn't answer. "It's a Chevrolet. I'll bet it's dark green," she said triumphantly. "And I know who drives it: Hot and Sweet." She brushed its fender lightly with the tip of her finger. "You wait. When you get your prints done, you'll find a dent right there. And here in the corner of the windshield will be a crack. It'll be barely discernible, but if you'll look closely, you'll see it."

She was unprepared for Matt's response. His good arm clasped her tightly around the waist as he swung her into a circle. "Maybe we do have a clue after all. You're great! I didn't know I had a female Sherlock Holmes on my hands."

Sara laughed. "I only hope I'm right," she said breathlessly.

That night, Sara turned restlessly in her bed, her mind seething with questions. Did Hot and Sweet really fit into the accident and the intrusion of their home? Was there a connection between him and Brad? And what about the mysterious blond fellow?

She looked at the red numbers on her clock. A sinking sensation rolled inside her. It was eleven-thirty. Dad had called it "prime time for excitement around here."

"I'm being silly," she whispered. She pulled her blanket up under her chin, but her uneasiness persisted. Tossing her covers off, she walked barefoot to the window.

The dark bulk of the rhododendrons and ivy was still, the street empty in the night. Sara's frog friends croaked their repetitive messages, and she smiled.

Sara stiffened, aware of a tense electricity in the air. Her questing gray eyes probed the night.

A police car cruised down the darkened street. It slowed in front of the house, speeded up, and was gone.

Sara remained motionless, her thoughts darting like birds searching for insects. The hedge branches stirred, and a large dark shape moved onto the sidewalk.

Sara's hands trembled as she gripped the window ledge. She leaned forward, peering into the darkness.

It wasn't human. Her mouth dried, and she licked her lips. A sudden muffled laugh rose above the pounding of her heart. Boris?

Sara rushed from her room and flew down the steps. She stepped onto the porch calling softly, "Boris! Boris!"

He came toward her from the shadows of the great oak guarding the street, his big tongue lolling, his tail wagging. "You silly creature," Sara chided as he came close. Affection stirred inside her as she put both hands on his huge forehead.

"You're supposed to be watching out for us, not wandering into the street. What happened anyway? Did someone leave the gate unlatched?"

Sara looked down at her sleepshirt. "I'm not going out

like this, Boris. Come inside." She opened the door wide and Boris followed her.

"You can sleep in here and risk Mom's wrath," she said, gesturing at the floor. "Make yourself comfortable."

Boris wasn't interested. He tucked his great muzzle into Sara's hand and looked entreatingly into her eyes.

Sara shrugged her shoulders and started up the stairs. Boris followed, his paws thudding on the steps.

At the door to her room she turned. "If you come in, you'll have to be a gentleman," she admonished. "You'll have to treat my stuffed cat right."

Boris seemed to understand. In dignified silence he stalked in and lay down on the floor at the foot of the bed.

He put his massive head on his outstretched paws and regarded her unblinkingly. Sara smiled at her hulking companion, then crawled into bed. As she turned out the light, the frogs started croaking louder.

Boris's breathing mingled with their croaks, and Sara's eyes grew heavy. She could sleep now.

8

Matt laid the photos on the Faulkners' dining room table and stood back. "I'm sorry, Sara," he said. "There isn't much. No license plate number, no cracked windshield—nothing but that dented fender."

Sara peered at the photo beneath his finger. "You're right," she agreed. "The crack doesn't show at all."

"It's a common enough place for a car to have a dented fender," Matt reminded her.

The eagerness that had swelled so quickly inside Sara when Matt stepped onto her front porch dipped low. "It's probably just coincidence," she said softly. "But Officer Peterson is picking up the extra set of prints this afternoon anyway. Maybe he'll find something."

They stared at the photos in silence. "I have a surprise in the car for our lunch," Matt said after a while. "I'll go get it."

"Oh, Matt, you didn't have to. When I asked you over yesterday, I didn't expect—"

Matt grinned and leaned forward. One finger came up and tapped her lightly on the nose. "Shh."

"But Mom has pizza in the fridge. All we have to do is heat, eat, and enjoy. And if I know Mom, she'll come in any moment with store-bought cookies."

Matt's grin deepened into mystery. "This isn't store-bought," he said. "All you have to do is promise to eat."

Sara selected a photograph from the table and pretended to study it intently. "Well . . ." she began.

"Promise? I fixed it myself."

"Of course. Now go get it before I die an unnatural death."

Matt laughed and hurried out the door. His "Remember, you promised" drifted back to the dining room.

Sara smiled, then bent over the photos. She couldn't believe the Chevrolet wasn't Hot and Sweet's. But of course she couldn't prove it—not without the revealing cracks in the windshield.

She looked again at the fascinating old house. Its turrets and rounded windows lent a peculiar old-time charm.

"I have half a notion to go searching for you," she mused.

The door opened and in came Mandy and Mom, carrying groceries. "Ooh, pictures!" Mandy squealed. "Let me see."

"They aren't ours," Sara explained. "They belong to Matt—or rather, the camera I found." She picked up the house photo and handed it to her mother. "Have you seen this house before?"

Her mother frowned over the top of her brown paper bag. "No, not that I know of."

"We bought cookies, Sara," Mandy interrupted. "Yummy oatmeal and chocolate chip."

Matt stepped into the room, holding a glass bowl in his hand.

"And Grandma's molasses bars," Sara finished for her. She winked at Matt and he winked back, holding the bowl out to her.

She looked at its contents curiously. "What is it, Matt?"

Mandy and Mom crowded around eagerly.

"It's a wild salad that I gathered this morning," he explained. "It's a little late in the season, but I found Miner's lettuce, yellow violet leaves—we call them Johnny-jump-ups—"

Mandy touched a thin, elongated leaf. "Is this a dandelion leaf?"

Matt looked at her approvingly. "It sure is. If it were a bit earlier in the season, I'd have put in fern fiddleheads. They're good."

"What do they taste like?" Sara asked.

"Um, a little like a raw green bean—only stronger. You'd have to taste one yourself to really know."

"Am I supposed to serve this wild salad?" Sara's mother asked dubiously.

Matt laughed, a clear, ringing laugh that seemed to have some of the sparkle of a mountain stream. "Sure," he answered. "It's good as is, or you can add a bit of dressing. Italian tastes great on it."

Mom shook her head as she opened the refrigerator. "Dandelions and Miner's lettuce." Removing a large pizza from the shelf, she set it on the counter and laughed. "What a combination—junk food and wild delicacies."

"Pizza's not junk food," Sara retorted. "It has lots of good, high-quality protein, tomatoes—"

"And sausage and olives and cheese," Mandy chimed in. "Hurry up, Mom. I'm starved."

Matt and Sara set the table with red-checked napkins and plain white plates, while Mom and Mandy scurried around the kitchen, readying lunch.

Sara stepped back from the table, smiling approval at its cheery appearance. "Your salad looks pretty enough to be a centerpiece, Matt."

Matt cocked his head to one side. "It sure does."

"No way," Mandy protested. "We need flowers." She dove for the drawer which held the garden shears and brandished them in the air. "Matt and I will get them."

"Oh no, you won't," Mom intercepted. "You're helping

me." She handed the shears to Sara. "Would you? Dad's garden is flourishing, and it's a shame to keep it all outside."

Sara nodded and took the shears. "I'll go with you," Matt volunteered.

The two tripped down the stairs and into the side yard. A soft breeze ruffled their hair and brought the sweet scent of honeysuckle to their noses. Matt sniffed and looked around appreciatively.

Red and white roses spilled over the fence, vying with the prolific grape vine for a place of importance. The beds in front sported a glorious profusion of deep blue delphiniums and red and white snapdragons.

"That's it!" Matt cried. "A bit of blue—"

"And red and white," Sara finished for him. She stepped to the edge of the lawn and selected several long-stemmed snapdragons and a single tall delphinium. For a moment, she peered into its white-starred center.

"I'd like to draw it," she said, "just the way it is."

Matt's eyebrows darted up. "You draw?"

A slight flush tinted Sara's cheeks. "Just simple things really—like leaves, mushrooms. I'm not much good."

"I'd like to see them, Sara."

Sara nodded, then abruptly changed the subject. "About the cars, Matt. What do you think they mean?"

Matt shook his head. "I don't know. Maybe whoever took the pictures has a weird hobby."

The window above their heads slid open. "Pizza's ready. We'll give you five minutes," Mandy called. She hung out the window, her long blond hair dangling, a mischievous smile lighting her elfin face.

Little pest, Sara thought. "We'll be right there," she called, starting up the porch steps.

Matt stopped her. "Your tunnel," he said. "I'd like to see it."

Sara turned, confusion tangling her thoughts. "Why?"

Matt shrugged. "Just curious. I happen to like tunnels."

Sara's eyebrows drew together in a question.

Matt laughed. "I have a tunnel," he explained. "It's in the woods and it's beautiful. It must have been a road once, but now it's overgrown with all kinds of things—honeysuckle, wild roses. Wild things hide there. Birds, butterflies, chipmunks—"

"Our tunnel isn't like that at all, Matt," Sara interrupted. "Our house is old. We don't use the tunnel now, but at one time it was the service entrance to the street."

She sighed and shook her head. "It's ugly, Matt. Just old gray cement."

"And ivy," Matt said. "I've seen it waving around the opening."

"Sara! Matt!" Mandy called.

"Coming!" Sara shouted. Her fingers tightened around her flowers as they hurried up the steps and into the house.

The bright bouquet, coupled with the tangy wild salad, made lunch a fun event. *Or was it Matt's company?* Sara wondered. He was different. Something in his personality drew her—not the way Brad had. This was something equally exciting, and somehow better.

After lunch Sara and Matt walked out to Matt's pickup. "I appreciate your taking me to work," she said as she got in and set her purse on the dented floorboards.

"It's my last day, you know," she confided. "Mom begins her job at the bridal shop next week."

"Glad?"

Sara frowned thoughtfully. "Yes, I am. I feel relieved." She twisted her collar. "I want to start a quiet time, too, Matt. Ever since I saw that picture of your mossy stump, I've felt like trying it."

Matt flashed a huge grin. "It's the best thing that's ever happened to me," he said. "Taking time for God gives my whole day more purpose. Except sometimes I think the pressures are greater."

"What do you mean?"

"My youth pastor explained it rather well I think. He said that Satan becomes more active when he sees us giving God first place. He read us a verse that really encouraged me, though. It says 'the one who is in you is greater than the one who is in the world.' "

Sara rummaged through her purse for a pencil. "Where do you find that?" she asked, pulling out a stubby pencil and small note pad. "I might begin my first quiet time there."

"First John 4:4," he said, glancing sideways. The clump of flowers decorating the notepaper's edge caught his attention. "Did you draw that?"

Sara quickly covered her sketch.

"But it's great," Matt protested. "Please, could I see it?"

Sara uncovered the paper reluctantly. "It's just something I play around with."

"Wild Camas!" he exclaimed. "And you a city girl."

"Lots of wild things grow in the woods along Terwilliger Boulevard," Sara said. "I go there a lot. Sometimes with Mandy, sometimes alone."

"Any mossy stumps available?" Matt teased.

"I wasn't thinking *that* especially. But maybe it is a good idea—a quiet place away from the house."

Matt nodded. "The place isn't what's important, though," he said. "It's taking the time to be with God that makes the difference—and doing it every day. For me that means setting a time."

Sara looked up. "Which is?"

"Nine in the morning, right now. I'm working afternoons and evenings."

"Nine o'clock," Sara mused. "I wonder—"

Matt grinned. "Want to join me? That's how my friend

Russ and I helped each other get going. We were separated by miles but we made a point of having our quiet times at the same time."

Sara nodded. She put her note pad inside her purse and looked at him. His tanned hands gripped the wheel. A light blue shirt, open at the neck, exposed his tanned neck. His brown hair waved naturally.

He's good-looking enough to be one of those outdoorsmen in the commercials, she thought. Then he turned, and the gentleness around his mouth banished her illusion. *He sure knows God,* she thought, *I wish I did . . .*

The Burgermill was already a flurry of activity when Matt dropped Sara off a few minutes later. Immediately, the rush absorbed her as she took orders and collected money.

Customers kept her too busy to think of quiet times, or mossy stumps, or old houses and cracked windshields for that matter.

Toward evening, she looked out the window and saw the familiar green Chevrolet. Hot and Sweet's gaze caught hers at once. He closed one eye in a long, suggestive wink.

Sara's heart jumped and fluttered in her throat. To distract herself, she looked at the windshield, then at the dented fender. Neither defect was visible.

She clasped her hands together, the lifted her chin with quick courage.

Hot and Sweet watched her with a dark glint in his eye. "Aha, sweetheart. Miss High Hat's down from her pedestal."

"Not really," Sara said quietly. "I just wanted to ask you something."

"Ask on. I'm at your command."

His look was intense. Sara held her ground. She gestured toward the windshield. "What happened to the crack?" she asked.

The smile faded from Hot and Sweet's face. Something dark and formidable touched his eyes. "Never was a crack," he said. "What made you think there was?"

Sara tossed her head in unbelief. "There was," she said. "And I don't see why you should deny it. And the fender—" she pursued. "The dent is gone."

The scowl on Hot and Sweet's face deepened. "You're imagining things," he said brusquely, "mixing my car up with someone else's."

"I'm not," Sara persisted. "How long have you been driving it, anyway?"

Hot and Sweet's hand shot out and clasped her wrist.

"Let me go!" Sara cried.

"Not unless you tell me what you're getting at," he hissed.

Sara felt her heart plunge from her throat into her stomach. For a moment, she thought she would lose her lunch. A memory of Matt saying, "the one who is in you is greater than the one who is in the world," flashed through her mind. Courage returned, and she remembered something. *Dad's been looking for someone to take out the dents in our back fender.*

She smiled sweetly at the angry man. "I was wondering where you got your body work done. My father is looking for somebody reliable to do work on our car." She waved her free hand airily.

His scowl deepened, and he tighted the grasp on her wrist.

Doubt mingled with her unanswered questions. What *was* she getting at anyway?

"I wonder," she murmured, "maybe it was another green Chevrolet—same year, but the color could have been darker. . . ."

The clasping fingers released her. His angry look seemed to fade as he looked at her. "How'd you like to go for a ride?" he tempted. "We could run up to the restaurant on Skyline Boulevard. Have a Coke—"

Sara smiled gently. "Other plans," she replied. "Sorry." She started to turn away, but Hot and Sweet stopped her.

"My order," he protested.

A warmth crept into Sara's cheeks. "Sorry."

As she handed him his order, he licked his lips. "Remember, I like my coffee hot—and sweet." The suggestive leer rose into his eyes, and Sara drew back.

When she looked again, the green Chevrolet was heading out of the lot, its movements quick and jerky. Then it was gone, but not before Sara observed the license plate number. She wrote it on the back of an order pad—AGC 540.

9

Tangled roses clambered over the fence, their white blooms striving to imitate the snowy clouds scattered in the morning sky. Blue delphiniums stretched heavenward.

Like me, Sara thought, *trying to reach out to my Creator.*

She sat on the bench in the side yard, her open Bible on her lap. Boris lay beside her, his huge muzzle resting on her feet, his bright eyes darting from flower to flower.

Boris lifted his head abruptly. Sara turned to follow his gaze.

A robin crouched in the grass, its neck pulled in, wings half-spread like a tiny helpless kite. Sara put her Bible on the bench and walked toward the bird, Boris close behind her.

The bird lifted its head and tensed. Then it beat its wings on the ground and lifted into the air.

"It's her leg, Boris," Sara explained. "See how it dangles?"

They went back to the bench. Sara sat down and picked up her Bible. Boris folded his huge legs beneath him, resuming his former pose.

Absently, Sara reached out and smoothed his muzzle. She looked up at the leaves of the great maple overhead.

"Lord," she murmured, "you seem so far away."

David felt like this, she recalled. *Somewhere in the Psalms he begged God not to be silent, not to be far from him.*

"I'm trying to reach out to God, Boris," she explained. But was she? Her thoughts kept racing to Matt, to the photos, to Hot and Sweet's hasty exit the night before.

She shook her head and thoughtfully began turning the pages, picking out a phrase here, a thought there.

Suddenly, the words from Psalm 34 jumped off the page at her, "The Lord is close to the brokenhearted and saves those who are crushed in spirit."

"Maybe that's what's wrong," she mused. "Perhaps if I'm to have a strong new me inside, I need to have a broken heart first."

The conviction grew within her. True, she was ashamed of the attraction she still felt at times for the handsome Brad, discouraged with her spiritual life that seemed like a yo-yo. But asking for a broken heart?

"I never thought about how it looked to you, Lord. I mean, I've been sorry, but I never really thought about how my sin makes you feel."

Pain stirred inside her. She remembered the story of the Shepherd searching for the lost lamb until He found it. She pictured Him gathering the lamb up in His arms, holding it close, then carrying it home on His shoulder.

"Poor, little lamb," she whispered. She underlined the verse in Psalms before she went inside. Her first day with Mandy was about to begin.

The two of them were dawdling over a late breakfast when the phone rang. Excitement tinged Sara's voice as she recognized Matt's deep tones.

"Hi, Matt. Anything new?"

"No, but would you and Mandy like to go to the pond with me?"

Sara's heart did a flip-flop, then quietly resumed its usual steady beat. "I'm not sure. I'd have to call Mom."

"And if she says yes?"

Sara laughed breathlessly. "Of course," she said. "Mandy would love it, too!"

Mandy's blue eyes widened as she looked up over the top of her glass of milk. "Love what?" she demanded.

"An outing at Matt's pond. You'd like it, Mandy."

Mandy set her glass down with a smack that threatened to shatter it. "To the pond!" she cried. "Now?"

Sara smiled and nodded. "I'll call you back, Matt." She hung up the phone and quickly dialed the bridal shop.

Mandy leaped from her chair and circled her arms around Sara's neck. "Tell her to say yes," she willed. "Please!"

Permission granted, Mandy whirled around the room. Sara rolled her eyes and dialed Matt's number.

"That's that," she said as she put down the receiver. "Matt will be here in an hour." She looked at her little sister critically. "You'd better change your blouse."

Mandy flew up the stairs two at a time and Sara cleared the table. It would be fun to explore Matt's pond, she decided, but most of all, it would be fun to be with Matt.

She tossed her dishrag into the sink and went upstairs. After she changed into her favorite jeans and blue plaid shirt, she went to the window and looked down at the side yard. She always marveled at the difference a bird's-eye view made. It almost made you want to be one.

"Mrs. Robin," she exclaimed, "you're back!"

The bird hunched down as she had before. As Sara watched, the robin turned, looked at the ground around her, cocked her head, then stabbed with her beak. An angleworm wriggled to get free.

Sara turned quickly to the drawer where she'd placed the camera. If she could just get a photo to show Matt . . .

She hurried down the stairs and out into the yard just in time to see the robin flutter a few feet to another spot. The bird stabbed again and another worm dangled in the air. Sara focused carefully and pressed the button. The camera clicked and elation filled her. She had captured the bird forever on film. This was almost as much fun as drawing flowers.

Sara moved forward, refocusing the lens. But the robin flew away.

Sara was undaunted. Carefully, she focused on a white-eyed delphinium, then a shadowed rose still shimmery with dew. She was still in the garden when Matt came, Boris and Mandy bounding beside him.

"Aha!" he exclaimed. "I see you've been bitten."

"Your photographs did it," she confessed. "I just hope this thing is set right."

Matt took the camera and examined it. "It's okay. They ought to turn out great." He handed it back to her. "You're on the last picture, though."

Sara gasped. "Already?" she moaned. "I was going to take it to the pond."

"I don't have extra film," Matt apologized. "But my camera's loaded. It's in the pickup."

"I'll leave this one here then," Sara said. "Wait. One last picture—"

She backed Mandy, Matt, and Boris against the roses and aimed. Matt laughed, stuck his head close to Mandy's and made a silly face. Sara tried not to giggle as she snapped the picture.

Hurriedly, she took the camera to her room and dumped it in the drawer. Then the three of them were off, packed together in Matt's father's old dilapidated pickup.

Matt didn't bother to apologize for his vehicle. "I'm kind of fond of this old thing," he confessed. "Dad's had it since I was a little kid."

They jounced down the street and onto the freeway. "It has a hard time keeping up," Matt said.

"I don't mind," Sara replied.

"Neither do I," said Mandy. "It's like an old man. Does it have a name?"

Matt laughed. "Funny you should ask. We call it Doc, after the dwarf in Snow White."

"Doc," Mandy mused, accenting it with her tongue. "Doc."

Sara thought Grumpy would be more appropriate.

As they left Portland behind, Sara told Matt about her encounter with Hot and Sweet. "I got his license plate number, too," she explained, "just in case."

Matt nodded. "That's good."

In spite of Doc's slow speed, they arrived at their destination in good time. They parked alongside the road and got out. Mandy, unable to contain her exuberance, bounded ahead, sailing over deep cow ruts and tufts of grass. Matt sprinted close to her and grabbed her hand.

"Slow down, young'un," he entreated. "If you burst through here like a two-ton truck, you'll scare the wildlife away."

Reluctantly, Mandy slowed her pace to match the speed of the other two. "Are there really ducks here?" she asked. "And water skippers?"

Matt swung her hand cheerily. "Sure are. And salamanders, too."

"Ugh," Sara groaned. "They're so ugly!"

Matt caught her hand in his, and the three of them walked together. A warmth that rivaled the midday sunshine grew within Sara. She smiled up at Matt, restraining an urge to give his hand a squeeze.

They stopped at the top of the hillock and looked down. The pond lay peaceful in the slight hollow, green meadow grass before it, a tangled mass of fern and trees beyond.

Slowly, they moved through the grass dotted with cowpies. White sweet clover and yellow buttercups smiled up at them. Purple foxgloves fringed the edges of the hollow, an occasional clump scattered among the other meadow flowers.

Matt let go of Sara's hand and scooped a foxglove into his palm. "See these tiny holes below the stem? Hummingbirds do that when they suck nectar."

Sara looked at the tiny holes in awe. "Really? I thought they were poisonous."

"It is, in large quantities. But in smaller doses, it's used as a heart medicine. Apparently, the birds don't get enough to harm them." He gestured toward the water. "Look."

The murky water rippled faintly with the movement of dipping flies, darting water skippers, a jumping fish. Even as they watched, a male mallard left his wild snowball and willow cover to swim toward the center of the pond.

Mandy hopped with excitement, waving her pointing finger. A large brown turtle sunned himself on a partially submerged log. Before they could come closer, he slipped into the water and disappeared.

Mandy could contain her silence no longer. "It was real!" she cried.

She sat down and pulled off her shoes and socks, then swiftly rolled up her blue jeans. Sara and Matt grinned at each other as they watched her wade into the squishy mud dotted with tall pond grass.

Matt nodded toward a dilapidated dock jutting out into the water. "Shall we?"

They walked together onto the sagging boards. Matt picked up a long stick and prodded a dark area in the water. A golden salamander surfaced, grabbing an apparent tidbit before vanishing again into the dark muck.

"I still think they're ugly," she said.

She looked across at the other shore. Wild pink roses and snowballs, their blossoms past their prime, hung over the water.

She left the dock behind and turned toward the meadow, Matt beside her. A tiny blue flower winked up at her like a forgotten star.

"Wild forget-me-not," Matt answered before she could ask.

Sara watched a blue dragonfly sail low, noted a pair of swallows dipping in dance above the foxgloves.

Matt took his camera from its case and focused on a blackberry vine festooned with white blossoms and golden honeybees. He walked farther away and Sara was left alone absorbing the trill of an unseen bird and the whisper of the wind in the firs.

Suddenly she had an idea. *I'll find some flowers to sketch.* She picked a tall foxglove marked with a hummingbird kiss. Carefully, she snipped off a blue forget-me-not.

Mandy left the mud and climbed up beside her. "Oh," she exclaimed, "a tiny strawberry!" Then it was gone, popped into Mandy's mouth.

"I'm going to take these home and draw them," Sara said as Matt came toward her.

"Great." Matt ran his hand over his camera. "I captured a couple of pictures that I think will be special. One was a maidenhair fern dripping over the water; the other, believe it or not, is that wild blackberry vine. It has a certain look to it."

Sara smiled. She felt she could have stayed forever in this quiet haven.

But Matt had to work that afternoon. He dropped his hand onto Mandy's head and started toward the pickup.

The drive back to town seemed too short. It was hard to face the old uncertainties after the idyllic morning.

When Matt stopped the truck in front of the house, Mandy jumped out and raced ahead in her usual impetuous manner, letting herself through the gate. Her dismayed cry brought Sara and Matt running.

She stood on the steps, an arm around Boris. He stood tall, yet seemed ashamed, his neck bare of his spiked collar. The front door gaped open.

"Not again!" Sara cried. "It can't be—"

They rushed through the door. The living room brooded silent and empty, the kitchen untouched. But upstairs in Sara's room, drawers were upturned on the floor and bed.

"The camera," Sara cried. "It's gone!"

10

Once again the Faulkner house teemed with action.

"I won't have it!" Mr. Faulkner exclaimed as he came in the front door. "We should be able to get protection from this kind of trouble."

Sara couldn't have agreed more. "But, Dad," she said, "it could have been worse. This time nothing was taken—except the camera I found, and Boris's collar."

Her father's fist slammed onto the edge of the table. "That collar is what makes me so mad. They were using Boris to flaunt their power right in our faces."

The doorbell chimed softly, and Sara jumped.

"It's just Officer Peterson," Mom soothed. "I called him as soon as you told me about the camera and collar."

Dad opened the door. "Thanks for coming so quickly."

Officer Peterson nodded, his eyes searching the room. "Sara," he said, "are you okay?"

"Yes," she replied, grateful for the concern in his eyes. "But the camera is gone—the one I found at the accident scene. Dad, will you take him upstairs and show him where I had it?"

The two men disappeared up the stairs together. Matt and Sara went into the kitchen.

"I hate thinking of someone in my room, going through my things," Sara said. She opened the fridge and took out two Cokes.

Matt and Sara sat down at the table, sipping their

Cokes in silence. Sara's thoughts kept returning to her room. Would something else turn up missing? What *was* happening, anyway?

She turned as her father and the policeman stopped inside the door.

Officer Peterson was encouraging. "I think this will be the last time, Sara. Somehow, I think you're onto something with that camera. I'm not sure what—"

Matt agreed. "Now that they have it, it's unlikely they'll be back."

But Sara shook her head. "They still don't have *their* film," she said. "They'll discover soon enough that the film inside the camera isn't the roll they want."

There was silence as each person digested the information.

Officer Peterson frowned. "I'll assign an extra patrol car. In the meantime"—he looked hard at Mandy—"keep an eye on the little one."

After he left, the rest of the family gathered around the table. Mr. Faulkner turned to his wife. "You'll have to stay home tomorrow. We can't have these girls here alone."

She nodded regretfully. "I agree," she said softly. "I'll call Lucille and explain."

"What about Aunt Nina?" Mandy asked. "Didn't you say she wanted to come and spend a month with us sometime?"

Mom's eyebrows arched. "Why, Mandy, I think you might have something there."

Aunt Nina was delighted that her niece needed her. Alone, her two children grown and her husband gone, it was exactly right for her.

The Faulkner house exploded with a different kind of activity. Even though Aunt Nina was partially handicapped and used a cane, she was never still.

She roasted chickens and baked bread. She washed windows, cleaned closets, and set the girls doing innumerable errands.

"No one would dare come near our house with Aunt Nina in it," Mandy grumbled, her arms loaded with jars for the basement shelves. "They wouldn't dare."

Sara looked out the sparkling clean window. Boris lay on the porch, his head on his paws, the picture of a neglected dog.

"Daddy should have gotten Aunt Nina instead of Boris in the first place," Mandy continued. "No one would dare take a spiked collar off *her* neck!"

"Mandy!" Sara reproved. Her lips twitched with suppressed laughter. She could imagine her Aunt Nina meeting Brad at the door, broom in hand. He'd back up for sure, probably falling over Boris in the process.

"Go put your jars away, Mandy," she said.

Mandy stomped down the stairs. Sara could still hear her grumbles as she went out to join Boris on the porch. He looked up at her hopefully, his great tail thumping the wide boards.

"I'm sorry, Boris," she said. "Maybe when this is all over we'll get back to normal. Then you can sleep in my room."

She rubbed his ears thoughtfully as she remembered the afternoon she had stood and looked at her ransacked room. It *had been* horrible. But Sara had to admit, it had been freeing, too.

The mental vision of Brad upturning her lingerie drawer and touching her personal items had made anger swirl inside her. Never again would a look from his dark eyes release butterflies in her stomach. Never again would he find her stumbling in his footsteps, reduced to a helpless blob of compromise. She was free.

Except for Aunt Nina.

It was hard to find a quiet moment with Aunt Nina's restless spirit dominating the house. Sara had begun rising early for her quiet time in the side yard.

Her robin was still there—plump, bright-eyed, intact except for the one leg that dangled helplessly. She stood in the grass, peering, thrusting with her beak, feeding, then fluttering forward. Sara marveled at her quiet courage and perseverance.

"She's a good illustration of what it is to be patient," Sara told Boris who was stretched at her feet.

Boris lifted his head, nodded and lay back down, quietly watching the fluttering bird. He never bothered it. Once Sara saw him lunge at a neighboring cat lurking too close. She wondered if the huge dog and the small bird had some unspoken agreement between them.

Sara smiled. "You're a good dog, Boris. A little large, but a good dog just the same."

The telephone shrilled and Sara hurried into the living room.

"It's for you," Aunt Nina said, holding the receiver out to her. "Matt."

Sara took it. "What's up, Matt?"

"My bandage is off and my motorcycle's fixed," Matt said joyfully. "Want to go for a ride with me?" His voice lowered, "We could go house hunting."

Sara laughed. A picture of the turreted house in the photograph leaped into her mind. "I'll have to ask."

Aunt Nina stood in the doorway, a dish towel flung over her shoulder, her legs braced. For a moment the thought of Boris's spiked collar encircling her neck made Sara's lips quiver. It would have been so fitting.

"Matt wants me to go for a motorcycle ride with him, Aunt Nina. If I get permission from Mom or Dad, could you watch Mandy?"

Aunt Nina snorted disdainfully. "Who's watching out for whom?" she grumbled.

"Why, you are, Aunt Nina," Sara said meekly. "We couldn't have gotten through this week without you."

Aunt Nina's taut shoulders relaxed. "Don't bother to call your parents, honey. Just tell him yes." She stomped into the kitchen mumbling, "Motorcycle riding—in my day it was Saturday afternoons at the movies."

Sara giggled. Having Aunt Nina in the house wasn't all bad.

Sara was waiting on the porch when Matt roared to a stop. She ran out to him, eagerness flashing from her gray eyes.

Matt grinned back, noting with obvious approval her blue jeans, navy jacket, and plaid flannel shirt. "I'm glad you dressed warmly," he said.

He handed her a helmet and showed her how to fit it over her head and fasten the clasps beneath her chin. Then they were off, the wind pushing hard against Sara's visor, jacket, and jeans. It took a while for her to relax—especially with her arms around Matt's waist. But after a few miles she felt comfortable. It was fun!

Matt slowed for a corner and turned to her. "Like it?"

"Yes! Except for the noise!"

"You'll get used to it!"

They left Sara's neighborhood behind and began to explore an area with tall, old-fashioned houses. Matt slowed. Intently, they studied each house, searching for tall turrets and narrow rectangular windows.

Matt pointed to a tree bending over a tall, white-columned porch. "That tree looks like the one in the picture," he shouted, "But the porch is all wrong!"

A car careened around them and momentarily distracted Sara.

"He's in a big hurry, Matt," she noted. "Watch him!"

Her arms suddenly clutched Matt tightly. "Matt, that license plate. It's the one I wrote down at the restaurant!"

"Are you sure?" Matt twisted the throttle and the motorcycle jerked forward.

"The car is different," she gasped, "but the number is the same. I know it is!"

Her words were lost as Matt accelerated. The car was just ahead of them now, a bright yellow-and-black Plymouth. Sara peered through her visor. All she could see of the driver was his dark, well-shaped head. He turned to one side and Sara felt sure it was Brad. Or was it?

Her thoughts raced. What was the license plate from Hot and Sweet's Chevrolet doing on this car? She caught her breath as the motorcycle bore close to the Plymouth's rear bumper. The driver seemed unaware of their interest, intent only on hurrying through town.

He turned a corner and Matt followed. A red light loomed overhead, catching their cycle, but allowing the black-and-yellow car to go free.

Matt leaned toward her. "I'm still going to follow. I want to see where he goes."

The light changed, and the motorcycle jerked ahead. For a while Sara was afraid the speeding Plymouth had eluded them. Then she spotted it a few blocks ahead.

The chase continued through the tree-lined streets and onto the freeway out of town. Matt opened the throttle wide. The noise roared in Sara's ears. Her head began to throb. She leaned forward, pressing her face against Matt's shoulder.

She was unaware of which exit they took off the freeway, but when she lifted her head, they were on a winding country road. The black-and-yellow Plymouth flashed ahead, like a goldfinch darting into the wind.

Sara knew then that the dark-headed driver was aware of them and trying to elude them. Her stomach sank as they whirled around each curve. The Plymouth suddenly roared onto a lonely gravel road to the left.

Matt braked and tried to follow. But the loose gravel caught the wheel. They spun to a stop inches from the side of a tall bank.

"We lost him!" Matt exclaimed. He jumped off the cycle and turned to help Sara. She got off stiffly. An unexpected trembling traveled through her body. She hoped Matt wouldn't notice.

But he did. Gently, he helped her fumbling fingers with the clasp on her helmet. He removed it and led her to the side of the road.

"I'm sorry, Sara," he apologized. "That was a rough ride. I shouldn't have."

Sara licked her dry lips and swallowed hard. "It's all right, Matt. I wanted you to chase him as much as you wanted to. Where are we, anyway?"

Matt waved his hands vaguely. "Up in the hills. I'm not sure where myself. But don't worry. I'll get you home."

A chill made Sara shiver. "I almost hate to get back on," she confided.

Matt nodded. "We'll wait, then go slowly. I'm sorry." He reached out and touched her hand. "You're still cold."

He took her hand in both of his and began to rub gently. "Feel better?"

"I'm all right," Sara insisted, "really I am."

She gave him a wobbly smile that tried to reassure him but somehow failed. Matt's arm crept around her shoulder. Sara buried her face in his jacket and burst into tears.

They sat there a long time. After a while, Sara looked up. "I'm all right now, Matt." Her throat threatened to stiffen into a sob. She forced a smile. "We'd better go."

They walked together to the motorcycle and put on their helmets. But before Matt pulled her visor forward, he bent down and kissed her forehead.

"That's a promise," he said, "that I'll get you home safe and sound. No more wild rides."

Then he patted her cheek. "And that's a promise that we'll both come back. I have a feeling it would be good for us to look around these hills. We just might find that yellow-and-black Plymouth."

Sara felt like adding, "And Brad?" but she didn't.

11

Sara lay in bed, too tired to sleep. Visions of motorcycles and speeding yellow-and-black cars flashed through her mind. So did endless curves, driving wind, and—a warm arm drawing her close.

She sighed and turned restlessly onto her side, pulling her knees to her chest. The ride back into town had been long but carefree. They'd stopped at a wayside cafe and enjoyed a Coke, then explored a stream at a quiet rest stop. Before they got home, clouds had built up in the sky.

Sara could hear the wind's curious fingers probing her windowpanes. With the first gentle rain spats, the frogs in the pond began to rejoice.

"Silly frogs," Sara reproved. She stretched her legs out long and again felt their weighty weariness. The wind and rain and frogs soothed her. Sleep came quietly, gently, wrapping its dark cloak around her tired spirit.

Toward morning Sara dreamed. A tall house with turrets that cut into the sky rose before her. She walked toward it, even as sudden thunder growled and lightning bounced off its peaked roof. She stopped.

Aunt Nina's voice drifted up the stairs, accompanied by the steady banging of two metal objects. "You girls going to sleep your lives away? It's after nine and time to be moving! Look alive!"

Sara sat up, reluctantly pushing back her blanket. *After nine, and I promised Matt—*

She looked out the window. Thick clouds, tinted lavender from the thin, drawn curtain covered the sky, blotting out the mountain. She shivered. *Rain.*

There was a light tap on her door. The door opened and Mandy pranced in, somewhat like a pony, her head thrown back, her feet dancing as though she walked on rubber.

"Mandy!" Sara cried. "Where did you get that blouse? Take it off at once!"

Mandy bounced to a stop and frowned.

Sara felt sick as she looked at her. Mandy's innocent loveliness hid behind heavily blushed cheeks and bright red lipstick, her large blue eyes outlined with dark shadow. The black silk blouse Sara had tossed into the back of the closet mocked her with painful memories. Somehow, Mandy had managed to tuck and smooth it until it clung to her girlish figure.

"You've been in my room," Sara stormed, "and you look . . . terrible."

Mandy ran to her. Tears slid down her cheeks, making rivulets in her makeup. "I'm sorry, Sara," she cried. "I woke up early this morning and couldn't go back to sleep. I didn't have anything to do, so I came in here. And the next thing I knew—"

Sara hugged her little sister hard. "It's all right, Mandy. It's just that . . . I hate to see you dressed like that since . . . since . . ."

"I'll take it off," Mandy promised. She hugged Sara then ran out the door.

Sara dressed slowly, reluctant to face the dreary morning. She shivered and sat down on the edge of the bed instead, reaching for her Bible and opening to the fifteenth chapter of John. After a while she put her Bible aside and closed her eyes, trying to pray. Instead, she saw the house in her dream rearing into the clouds.

Sara's eyes popped open. "That's it!" she exclaimed. "We'll go house hunting. Mandy will love it!"

Mandy did.

Even Aunt Nina approved. "It'll do her good to go traipsing about with her big sister. Why, when I was a girl—"

Sara and Mandy caught each other's eye and winked.

After nearly an hour of poring over maps and outlining potential neighborhoods, the girls set out. "You look nice in that blue-checked shirt," Sara approved.

Mandy smiled. "Lots nicer than black silk, isn't it?"

Sara flushed and arched her eyebrows playfully. "What about me? Do I look better in turquoise blue than black?" She lifted her chin and turned a half circle.

Mandy cocked her head and regarded her soberly. "Yes, you do," she said. "That color makes your gray eyes almost blue.

Sara reached over and gave her a playful pat on top of her blond hair. "You're an observant little girl," she said. "I think you're just the person I need to spot that old house."

Mandy took Sara's words seriously. She sat on the bus with the picture on her lap, memorizing each detail.

"That big tree in the yard sort of leans toward the house, doesn't it?" she observed. Then a little later, "There are curtains on the main floor but not in the upstairs."

When the bus entered the neighborhood Sara and Matt had explored earlier, Mandy sat with her nose pushed against the window.

As the bus emptied, she stirred, "I don't see anything that looks like it at all. Why don't we ask the driver?"

Sara nodded and made her way to the front of the swaying bus. The driver looked at the picture with interest as she held it out to him.

"No—not around here. But wait . . ." He scratched his head thoughtfully. "Have you ever looked in the Glisan District out in northeast Portland?"

Sara shook her head. A few minutes later, with transfers in hand, they caught another bus.

"This is fun!" Mandy exclaimed. "You can see so much more than when you're going through in a car."

Sara agreed. But she was getting tired. Portland was so large, and there were so many out-of-the-way streets where a tall, ancient house could hide.

"It has to be a place where there are big trees," Mandy noted.

Sara looked thoughtfully at the maple-lined street. Something stirred inside her.

"Let's get out and explore."

Mandy stood up and Sara followed. She caught Mandy's hand as they jumped from the rear door onto the sidewalk.

"Let's go up that street," Mandy said eagerly.

The tall maples beckoned, rustling their leaves in invitation. Sara looked high above their branches and saw blue sky beginning to break through the clouds.

They started down the next block. The houses looked as though they had once been loved and cared for. But now an air of neglect prevailed. Sara noted a broken screen door, an unweeded flower bed, an old car parked in a driveway. All contributed to a general feeling of sadness.

Sara found herself wondering about the people living in the houses. Were they descendants of once well-to-do pioneer families? Or new families who could not afford to keep the neighborhood as beautiful as it once had been?

"The tree!"

Mandy's excited cry interrupted Sara's reverie.

They raced ahead, turning down another side street. There it was—a bit back from the street behind a tall, leaning maple, its rounded upstairs windows turned toward them, curtainless.

Excitement surged through Sara as she stared at the house. But her excitement mingled with a faint apprehension.

Mandy started to bound up the front walk.

"Wait!" Sara cried, plunging after her. She grabbed Mandy's hand, slowing her footsteps.

Would Brad come to the door? Sara wondered. Or the blond boy she'd seen at the accident scene? And what about Hot and Sweet? Would he show up here?

The girls stepped onto the front porch. "Maybe we should wait until Matt can come with us," Sara said nervously. She pushed a strand of brown hair off her forehead, then lifted her chin determinedly. It was broad daylight. There was nothing to be afraid of. Besides, she didn't need to hide behind a man's protection.

Sara bravely reached out and touched the doorbell. She could hear it ringing in the depths of the house.

No one answered. She tried again. Still no response.

"No one's home," Mandy whispered. "Let's look in the window."

"We shouldn't," Sara reproved. Then curiosity overwhelmed her.

They tiptoed over to the window and peered through the white, lacy curtains. A couch and chair. An open book before the fireplace. . . .

Sara gasped. "That vase," she whispered, "the one on the mantle. It looks like Mom's—the one that was stolen."

"Let's go inside and take it!" Mandy exclaimed. "They have no right—"

"Hush," Sara said. A car slowed on the street. She grabbed Mandy's hand. "Let's get out of here."

A sudden urge for action propelled them off the porch. For a moment Sara hesitated. Should they dodge behind the overgrown shrub or walk nonchalantly down the walk?

She chose the second option. With their pace held to a

saunter, Sara hoped they looked like neighbors out for a friendly afternoon visit.

No one seemed to notice. The car disappeared, the houses brooded in silence.

"Let's ask the next-door neighbor who lives there," Mandy suggested. "Maybe he knows something about these people."

Sara shivered nervously. "Oh, Mandy, I don't know—"

"Look!" Mandy cried. She pointed across the street. An elderly man leaned over the top of his shovel, arms folded, quietly watching them.

Sara's fingers tightened on Mandy's. "Don't point, Mandy. It's rude." She had a sudden impulse to give her little sister a quick kick, but stifled it. "Let's just go over and say hello."

Mandy's hands jerked to match her bouncing footsteps. "Maybe he can tell us—"

Sara shot her a warning glance. "You let me do the talking," she warned. "Hush!"

Sara pasted on a neighborly smile as they crossed the street. The man watched them, his gaze steady, though not unfriendly.

"Good afternoon," Sara called.

The gray head nodded, a faint smile creasing his face. "Afternoon's gone," he said regretfully.

The girls stopped. Sara gestured toward the house they'd just left. "No one's home."

"Ah, no," the old man mused. "Edna's gone visiting her sister in Tacoma. She won't be home until tomorrow or the day after. You relatives of hers?"

Sudden pink dyed Sara's cheeks. Mandy's fingernails dug into her sister's palm. "Not exactly . . ."

The old man frowned. "You stay away from Edna Schaffer's nephew, young lady. You hear? He ain't good news."

He thrust his shovel aside and turned away, his thin shoulders taut with indignation. Mandy and Sara looked at each other as the old man disappeared around the corner of the house.

"Brad," Sara murmured, "now I know where you live."

The girls walked back to the bus stop—but not before Sara turned to the towering house for one last look, one last promise.

"We'll be back when Edna Schaffer is home, old house. But next time, I'll be with Matt."

12

Matt's reaction to Sara's discovery of the old house was depressing. Or was it Aunt Nina's disapproving expression as she stood in the kitchen doorway that made Sara's spirits plummet?

"In my day, boys called girls," she said loudly.

Sara's cheeks burned. She clutched the receiver tighter, hoping Matt hadn't heard Aunt Nina's strident voice.

"It was clever of Mandy to find the house," Matt said softly. "But I've been thinking. What does it prove? They might just have liked the way it looked."

Sara wet her lips. "I . . . we . . . Mandy thought she saw mother's cut-glass antique vase—"

"Are you sure?" Aunt Nina snorted. "There are lots of cut-glass vases around." Her cane thumped across the tiled floor as she retreated back into the kitchen.

Sara breathed a deep sigh of relief.

"I think you should call Officer Peterson," Matt said. "Of course, they would need proof before they could go snooping around."

"Do you think maybe you and I could?" she asked. "I mean go back—snoop around ourselves."

A sudden silence hung between them. Sara could almost reach out and touch it. "Matt?"

"I'm here, Sara. Just thinking." His sigh winged over the line and settled into Sara's heavy heart.

"Tomorrow is my day off," he said.

Sara's heart thudded with hope, which was soon dashed by his next words.

"What I'd like to do is to get away. The wildlife at the salt marsh is spectacular, and I haven't been there in ages. Tomorrow may be my only chance with that crazy schedule I have at work."

Disappointment stirred inside Sara. "That's all right, Matt," she said bravely. "I . . . I guess the old house will keep."

"It isn't the house I'm worried about, Sara. I need to go back to where we lost that yellow-and-black Plymouth. Something inside me tells me that's more important."

"Then why don't you? Go back, I mean."

Matt laughed. "Because the sandpipers are piping, and ducks are calling, and seagulls are flying, and I"—he lowered his voice theatrically—"must go," he said. "Want to go with me, Sara?"

Sara's pulse quickened. A day with Matt would be a day away from Aunt Nina's disapproval and Mandy's demands. But the house . . .

Sara longed to return to it. She was sure it contained her mother's missing camera and film, their stereo, the heirloom vase. She wanted to go back, but not alone. She needed someone with her.

An ugly thought twisted her stomach into a knot. Would they also find the tall, dark-haired boy whose attraction had begun all the trouble in the first place?

"How about it, Sara?" Matt was asking. "Do you think your parents would approve of a day's trip to the salt marsh? It's close to Nehalem Bay. We could get there in a few hours."

"I . . . I think so. Dad's beginning to act as though he trusts me—especially when I'm with you."

"Then how about it? We could take Mandy."

But I'd rather not, Sara wailed inwardly. *I'd rather it was just the two of us, alone. And I'd rather go to the old house.*

Aloud she said, "Oh . . . okay—I'll ask."

Matt didn't seem to notice her hesitation. "Great!" he exclaimed, "I'll call you tonight."

Sara, Matt, and Mandy stood together on a green, grassy knoll, the morning blue tipping around them. *It's like the inverted bowl you read about in books,* Sara thought.

"I camped overnight here once," Matt confided. "The next day I went down to the marsh and took some branches and covered a frame that the hunters use during duck season. I stayed inside most of one morning—duck watching."

"Did you really see them without them noticing you?" Mandy asked.

"Did I ever!" Matt made winging motions with his hands, and the three of them scurried down the path.

As they neared the bottom, salmonberry vines caught at their jeaned legs. A bird flew low over their heads, as intent as they to reach the open marshes.

Sara watched Matt ahead of her on the path. Sunshine streamed through the leaves and rested in a patch on his light brown hair. She caught her breath. She had never known anyone like Matt before.

A long blackberry vine clawed at her shoulder, drawing her concentration away from him. She withdrew the thorny tendrils carefully, observing the trees bordering the path. They were bound together with blackberry vines and nettles—an impenetrable, inhospitable place. Sara shivered and continued down the path.

Mandy galloped in the lead, her long, blond hair streaming below her shoulders. Sara pushed her own shoulder-length mop from her neck and blew at several stray hairs wandering by her nose.

She quickened her pace. Matt turned and looked back.

"You okay?" he asked, his smile radiant.

She nodded breathlessly. *He's glad to be in the woods,* she thought, *even though it's full of stinging nettles and thorns. It's where he belongs.*

They kept going until the nettle-bound woods were behind. The marshes, edged with driftwood and debris, lay before them. Matt bent over a rotting log patterned with blackberry leaves and white flowers.

"Sara," he called.

Overgrown salal waved, bending young green tendrils toward Sara, brushing her arm. "What is it, Matt?"

Matt knelt beside the stump as she joined him. Sara noticed another log ahead of him boasting tangled garlands of honeysuckle waving orange trumpets.

"Wow. They're perfect," she murmured.

But Matt wasn't looking at the flowers. His slim brown fingers untangled a fine gold chain from a branch. "It's a cross," he said with wonder. "Someone's lost a necklace."

Nostalgia moved inside Sara. She knelt beside him. "It's like the one I gave to Mandy." Their eyes met. "I shouldn't have."

She leaned back, bracing her hands on the soft earth bordering the path. Briefly, she explained why she'd given her cross to Mandy the night of his accident. "It just didn't go with what I was doing—sneaking out with someone I hardly knew—letting my parents down."

Matt nodded. "Isn't it funny how something like a cross necklace can be used to remind us of God when we need Him most?"

"Except I didn't want to be reminded right then. But you're right. It did make me feel lousy about what I was doing. It wasn't right. I sure wish I had that necklace now."

A faraway look came to Matt's eyes. "I carved a cross once and gave it to my brother. I was only ten. I always wondered if it meant anything to him. Especially later."

"Did he—"

"I don't know." The blue-gray eyes deepened into dark pools. "My brother isn't a Christian, Sara. He lives in Portland. He's into marijuana—alcohol . . ."

Matt's fingers touched the gold cross in his palm. "That's where I was going the night of the accident. He keeps moving from place to place, never telling us where he is—only occasionally getting in touch. That night he'd called."

"What does your brother look like? I mean—"

"Tall, skinny. When I was little I used to call him hawk-face. Made him so mad . . ." He turned.

Mandy, jumping from log to log, came toward them. "What are you two doing?" She spotted the cross lying in Matt's palm. "Oh," she said, one hand going to her neck. "It's beautiful—more beautiful than mine."

"It's for your sister," Matt said. He smiled at Sara, then leaned forward and clasped it around her neck.

Sara swallowed with difficulty. "Thank you, Matt."

The day now stretched before her with promise. It didn't matter that a faint rotting smell from the tide flats mingled with the fresh sea-salt smell, nor that Mandy pulled at her hand to make her hurry. This day was all she imagined it would be and more.

Sara knew the endless grass, the calling ducks, and the friendly clasp of hands would be tied together in her memory with a strand of gold—her new cross.

Twilight found the three of them—tired, dirty, and content—climbing back to where they'd parked the pickup.

"Whew!" Sara exclaimed as she and Matt leaned back against old Doc. Mandy wandered a short distance away and sat down, her face lifted toward the sky.

A silence fell over them as they watched the intense

blue of the sky being transformed into the pinkish purple color of flushed plums. Sara stared a long time before she realized there were stars hidden in its depths.

"First star I see tonight, I wish I may, I wish I might," she quoted, then paraphrased, "have the prayer I pray tonight."

"Sara," Matt's voice was as soft as the twilight. "I didn't want to say anything sooner, but something happened at our house last night—something we need to pray about."

Sara turned her attention from the gleaming golden star. "Yes?"

"Last night someone tried to break into my darkroom."

Sara gasped. "But that's impossible. How could they connect . . . us?"

"I wondered that myself. Then I thought of that yellow-and-black Plymouth we were following. He *could* have gotten my license number—somehow found out who owned the motorcycle. It's registered in my name."

"And you've been to my house. If they were snooping around—Matt, was anything taken?"

"Nothing. But they sure scared my mom to death. She was all alone when she heard this scrabbling noise. She thought it was the cat, and it made her mad. Nothing makes her more angry than a cat trying to get inside the house. And we have one like that." He laughed. "Sneaky—heads straight for the kitchen. Anyway, Mom got up to investigate, saw a light outside the window, and let out a yelp. Whoever it was, left."

"How awful," Sara said. She remembered her own fears in the night and shivered. Then another emotion rose inside her. "Does this mean that we'll check out that old house together soon?"

Matt nodded soberly. "Yes, it does." He shifted his arm until it rested behind her shoulder. "I should have gone back this morning to where we lost that Plymouth. Then we could go to that house tomorrow. But," he gestured wordlessly at the dying day.

"Mrs. Schaffer may not be home until later," Sara reasoned. "We'll get more information if we wait until we can talk to her."

"Maybe . . . but, Sara, I need to apologize. I was being insensitive about those break-ins at your house. I knew they were terrible, but I didn't realize how vulnerable they make a person feel. To have strangers actually inside your home, going through your things . . . your family is handling it well. I admire you."

A sudden lump swelled inside Sara's throat. "Not so very well," she whispered.

Matt's hand reached out and covered hers. "Sara, let's pray. Right now."

Sara nodded. "I've been reading that God is close to the brokenhearted. And now"—she searched for the right words—"I think I'm learning a little bit of what He meant."

She looked up at Matt in the pink dusk. His hand tightened over hers.

"Sara," he whispered, "there's something special about broken places, at least those God heals. Afterward, the broken spots are stronger than ever."

Hope as golden as the newborn stars overhead flooded Sara's being. She bowed her head to pray.

Memories of plum-colored skies wrapped around Sara as she snuggled beneath her covers that night. A deep peace curled itself around her spirit, born from more than the end of a perfect day—born from the prayer she and Matt had prayed together in the purple twilight.

That winking gold star had been far distant. *But God*

lives inside me, spreading comfort into all the nooks and crannies of my life, she thought.

Sara turned onto her side, pulling sleep around her like a blanket. Her last thought before slipping into dreams was, *He's here, right now.*

13

Sara opened her eyes to a morning devoid of purple twilight and golden winking stars. Aunt Nina's demanding tones hustled her into wakefulness before she was ready.

Aunt Nina can be irritating, she decided. *There isn't any way you can get around it.* Nevertheless, she pushed back the covers.

"The housework is always with us," she groaned to herself in the mirror. "Why all the rush?"

She dressed quickly. The sun-drenched morning inspired blue jeans, a candy-stripe blouse, and a gold clip to accent her brown hair. She touched the gold cross at her throat and smiled.

Household chores claimed her morning: breakfast dishes, vacuuming. It was midafternoon before Sara, Mandy, and a guilty-faced Boris skipped into the side yard.

"You're lucky," Mandy complained. "You get to go off with Matt while I"—her head bobbed toward the house—"I have to be here at *her* beck and call. I've a good mind to take a book and hide in the ivy tunnel."

A protest leaped to Sara's lips. "You wouldn't—"

Mandy shrugged and walked over to the grape vines rambling over the fence. "Actually, I could make a tunnel in here." She parted the leaves and peered inside. "Aunt Nina would never know."

Sara sighed and sat down on the wooden bench. Boris stretched at her feet, cradling his heavy head across her tennis shoes.

"It's after nine, Boris—way after. But I don't think God minds. I wish Aunt Nina—"

She opened her Bible to John 15 and read, "If you remain in me and my words remain in you, ask whatever you wish, and it will be given you. This is to my Father's glory that you bear much fruit, showing yourself to be my disciples."

Sara's gaze moved to the grape vine. "I'd like to bear that much fruit, Lord. I wonder if there are tiny, hard green grapes forming there now."

She sighed. "It takes time for them to grow, doesn't it? I wonder if it will with me—"

She closed her Bible and pulled out a spiral notebook. A grape leaf formed beneath her pencil, then an ivy leaf.

The slam of Matt's pickup door brought her to her feet. She grabbed her jacket, and the two rattled off.

Leaving the freeway, they began exploring unfamiliar, winding country roads. They hesitated at each curve, noting each crossroad.

Matt braked to a stop. "It was right here that he ditched us."

Sara nodded wordlessly, remembering the steep bank and Matt wiping away her stupid tears.

Matt's eyes darted eagerly from one side of the road to the other. "I don't think he realized at first that we were following him," he said.

"But, Matt," Sara protested, "I still don't understand what we're doing here, not really. What *are* we looking for?"

"I don't know." He flashed her a grin. "But the way that guy was driving, he knew these roads like I know my camera. Sara, that road to the left—let's follow."

He jerked the wheel and turned sharply. Vine maple and hazel branches scraped the sides of the pickup. Matt leaned over Sara and rolled up the window to keep the intruding branches from slapping her. "They sneak up on you," he explained.

He slowed the truck, easing it over the deep ruts and holes which tossed them from side to side.

"Don't worry about this road, Sara," Matt reassured. "Dad and I are explorers. I was raised on back roads like these."

An extra-deep rut thrust Sara's head to the roof, then jounced her firmly into the padded seat.

"Ouch!" she giggled. "You might have been raised on roads like these, but I . . . I'm lowered on them!"

After that it was hard to realize the seriousness of their mission. The pickup rocked with a fun-filled combination of laughter, ruts, and corny jokes.

They sobered as the road ended in an open field fringed with alders, willows, and towering firs. Cars in various stages of abandonment cluttered the meadow. They leered grotesquely at Matt and Sara, some devoid of headlights and bumpers, others without tires or fenders.

"Is this a junkyard?" Sara asked unbelievingly.

Matt shook his head and turned off the ignition. "I don't know," he said slowly, "but I'm going to find out." He opened his door and stepped out. Sara followed.

At the far end of the field towered a tall oak tree. A motor swung on a pulley from one stately limb. Matt and Sara walked toward it.

"Wow!" Matt exclaimed. "This is some place."

"Kind of spooky—"

"Not really. I wonder what this place is used for. Look, Sara. That old truck, it has a pulley on it, too."

Sara looked past his pointing finger. A strange contraption on the truck bed thrust its T-shaped nose into the air, the pulley dangling from one arm like a broken wing.

"I'm going to take a closer look," Matt said.

Sara held back uncertainly. "I'd rather we didn't. Somehow—"

Matt stopped. "Come on," he urged. "No one will care."

Sara shook her head. "It isn't that. Do . . . do you think this place has anything to do with . . . that yellow-and-black Plymouth . . . and Brad?"

Matt shrugged. "Hard to say. But it fascinates me."

"Someone has been here recently," Sara observed, noting the worn areas around the truck, the fresh tire tracks. "How long do you think these cars have been here?"

Matt didn't answer. He moved toward the truck, eagerness in the set of his shoulders. Sara watched him for a moment, then turned toward the car nearest her.

She peered through the windshield, trying to find the registration. But the car was only a gray shell. The seats were gone, the floor boards stripped, the steering wheel bare.

Sara backed away, lifting her eyes to the surrounding woods. An incline rose sharply to her left. "I bet I could see the whole yard from up there," she whispered. She could imagine herself telling Matt the number of cars and their exact locations.

She turned toward the hill and began to climb. At the top, she looked down. Cars of every description filled the clearing, spilling into the forest.

It's an eerie place, she thought. *Dead car bodies—skeletons . . .*

She moved down the other side of the hill, quickening her pace. The trees closed in around her. *Strange, here no one would ever dream that a car boneyard was close by.*

Afternoon sun slanted through the trees, making leaf patterns on the moss and brown fir needles. She could hear the rustling of leaves, the whir of tiny wings as a bird flashed past. She wandered farther into the forest.

The verses she'd read that morning about bearing fruit returned to her. She tipped her head back to look for fir cones. A tingle went through her as she discovered some small, hard, green cones not much bigger than her thumb.

The trees aren't struggling to grow them, she marveled. *They're just here—living, growing, producing what they were created to produce without struggle.*

She was so deep in thought that she failed to notice the sun dip behind the treetops. Wonder stirred in her as a soft, brown-feathered screech owl swooped low. It lit on a fir branch ahead of her and cocked its head.

Sara smiled. She advanced toward it softly, holding her breath. As she came within several yards of it, the owl flew away, lit on another branch, and peered down at her.

Again Sara moved forward. Again it flew. This time it disappeared, lost in the darkening woods.

Sara stopped, consternation filling her. Dusk was falling. She was far from Matt.

She turned to retrace her footsteps. After a while she stopped again. Was she going in the right direction? She looked up, but the trees stood like identical, silent sentinals wrapped in dusky aloofness.

Sara scowled. She noted vine maples clinging low to the ground, ferns brushing her jeans. They hadn't been there before, or had she not noticed?

"Am I really lost?" she whispered.

The soft wind sighing through the firs was her only answer.

Determinedly she went on. "I'm sure I came this way—or did I? Lord, I need help—your help." Her anxious eyes probed the woods. "There were alders and willows, I think. . . ."

Hope surged through her as she spotted the tiny leaves of a willow peeking out from behind a fir. Realization that the field was just beyond sent adrenalin rushing through her. She ran toward the clearing, then stopped.

Half-hidden by alder saplings and willow branches was a dark green Chevrolet with front windshield and fenders missing. She started to shout, "Matt!" then shut her lips. She moved forward slowly, softening her footsteps.

She had to look inside the car, see if she could discover if it had once belonged to Hot and Sweet.

A branch caught at her hair. A fallen limb tangled her feet. Still she crept forward. She stopped at the driver's side and looked in the window.

"It can't be," she whispered. "It can't be!"

She took a deep breath. Boris's spiked collar lay on the seat just out of her reach.

Cautiously, Sara looked around. The hulking shapes of nearby cars seemed to draw closer, menacing her. Fluttering shadows danced in the dusk.

Sara's hand reached out and woodenly clasped the door handle. It swung open. As she slid beneath the wheel she thought she heard the willow branches behind her move.

A twig snapped.

14

Sara's fingers closed over the spiked collar. Cold dread squeezed her heart. The burglar? Brad? Hot and Sweet? Any one of them could be near.

She squinted nervously through the darkening woods. No shadow lurked close, no sound but the gentle whisper of faintly moving willow leaves.

She opened her lips to call Matt, then closed them, reluctant to shatter the quiet. Clutching the collar with one hand, she reached for the door handle with the other.

It swung open and she jumped to the ground, her legs feeling like jelly. Her foot slipped.

A long arm from nowhere wrapped around her, pinning her arms to her body. Her tennis shoes skidded on the soft leaves of a downed willow branch. She almost lost her balance. Something tightened about her arms, jerking her back against a tree, and she dropped the collar.

Sara heard a mutter behind her. She twisted her body, trying without success to see her captor. Her lips opened in a cry only to be silenced as a twisted bandana gagged her mouth.

Her unseen assailant jerked the handkerchief into another knot, then quickly tied her hands to the tree. Picking up the spiked collar, he retreated, fallen branches crackling beneath his feet. Sara strained her ears and bent as far forward as the rope allowed.

Her heart thudded. Would he return? "Oh, Matt!" she

cried silently. "Where are you? Are you all right?"

Sinister silence, then a motor throbbed. Gradually the sound faded into the distance. The dark woods closed around her.

Sara trembled. If only she could break away and find Matt. She twisted her hands, her body, then sagged against the tree.

"Sara! Sara!" Was there panic in his cry?

A groan fought its way past the bandana. *Oh, Matt! I'm here*, her thoughts gasped.

He came toward her in the dusk. Then he was beside her, his fingers fumbling with the knot at the back of her head. The bandana dropped from her mouth.

"Matt!" she cried. Her hands strained against the rope.

"Don't," an unfamiliar voice said. "You'll make it tighter."

Sara tensed as his fingers grappled with the knot.

"I can't get it," he grunted. "Wait—" A slight pause, then, "I'm going to cut it with my knife. Hold still."

The cold knife blade pressed against her wrist. The rope slid from her hands.

She whirled around to face her rescuer. The long, hawklike face she'd memorized the day she found the camera looked down at her. She started to open her mouth, but he silenced her with a shake of his head.

"Please," he said, "don't tell Matt."

He turned and strode into the woods, his broad shoulders taut and squared. Sara stared after him, confusion tumbling inside her.

"Sara! Sara!"

This time she knew the tall figure coming toward her was Matt's own. She turned and ran to him. Then she was in his arms crying unintelligibly of spiked collars, unseen burglars, and unidentified attackers.

Matt held her gently, patting her shoulders. "Don't

worry," he reassured her. "Everything's going to be all right."

It took a while for Sara to regain her composure. "I know," she whispered. "It was just so scary. So . . ." She had a sudden desire to divulge the presence of her rescuer, but his "Please, don't tell Matt" restrained her.

Matt's arm tightened around her shoulder. "I know," he said. "But Sara, the pieces are beginning to fit together."

Sara rubbed the tears off her cheek with her palm and looked at him. "What do you mean?" she asked.

"After you wandered into the forest, I took a good look around. Sara, this is an illegal car-stripping operation. And—are you ready for this? I think the photos in the camera are evidence that these"—he waved his hand around the clearing—"are being made into new vehicles."

Sara nodded her head. "It makes sense, Matt." She suddenly remembered the spiked collar. "Boris's collar!" she exclaimed. "I found it." She related how she discovered it inside the Chevrolet parked beneath the willow.

She shuddered. "I think Hot and Sweet attacked me. Or Brad. The collar would link one of them to the break-in at our house, the camera, and eventually the accident."

Matt agreed. "That's probably why whoever hit my motorcycle took off so fast. They knew that if they stayed, the police would discover the car wasn't right. It looks like they forge registrations and everything. Of course, their plan is bound to have holes in it." He shuddered. "This whole thing looks pretty bad—dangerous, too." He looked behind him. "Let's get out of here."

"Yes, let's." She reached up a hand to squeeze the one lying protectively on her shoulder. "Thanks, Matt."

His hand closed over hers. "Come on, Sara."

With clasped hands they returned to Matt's pickup. On the way down the winding road, Matt turned to her.

"Sara, where did you go? After I'd looked that truck

over, I started to get frightened. You were nowhere around."

Sara smiled sheepishly. "First, I looked inside a car shell, then I decided to find out what I could see from the top of the hill. There was a screech owl," she confessed. "It kept flying from tree to tree—I followed it." She blushed.

Matt grinned his understanding. He turned off the steep gravel road and onto smooth pavement. "Shall we go to my house first? Take a look at those photos?"

Sara nodded. "Yes, let's. But, Matt, we still can't prove *who* tied me to that tree."

"No," Matt agreed. "Nor did you see who crashed into my motorcycle. But *they* don't know that."

Sudden fear closed around Sara's heart. "They've seen me, watched me. It makes me feel strange. . . ."

Silence filled the cab. Neither of them were willing to put the rest of their thoughts into words.

The night closed in around them. A golden star winked shyly from the top of a fir before disappearing into its branches.

Sara's star prayer breezed into her thoughts. *Star light, star bright, first star I see tonight, I pray I may, I pray I might, have the prayer I pray tonight . . . let us put a stop to these strange happenings—without anyone getting hurt. Please, Lord.*

The warm light spilling from the windows in Matt's house comforted her.

His mother welcomed them with a "Goodness!" as she led the way into the kitchen. "You two look worn out."

Sara nodded wearily as Matt took up the tale of the car-stripping operation in the woods. His mother gasped when he told how Sara had been tied to a tree.

"But that's awful!" she cried. "Terrible. We must report it right away!"

Matt shook his head. "First, we want to have a look at those photos again. Both Sara and I think they're important—maybe evidence against those involved in the illegal car stripping."

The three of them hurried into Matt's darkroom. Matt turned on the light and stepped to the table. His long, slender fingers leafed quickly through a pile of photographs beside the developing tank.

He frowned. "Mom," he said, "the photos aren't here. I was sure. . . . Did you move them? Put them somewhere?"

"I haven't been in here, Matt," his mother replied gently. "Could you have left them in your room?"

The frown deepened on Matt's forehead. "I was sure I left them here," he grumbled.

"Why don't you look in your room, Matt?" Sara suggested. "It's easy to misplace things."

"Especially if you're as absentminded as my son," his mother teased. Matt was still scowling as he left the room.

"I'm that way, too," Sara defended, "especially when I'm working on lots of things at once."

Matt's mother shook her head. "It doesn't seem to matter how few or how many. Matt walks around with his thoughts skyward. Sometimes I wonder—" She laughed suddenly. "I'm sorry, Sara. Matt *is* an unusual boy. And I appreciate him."

She smiled as her son rejoined them, but there was no answering smile from him. Worry darkened his face.

"Mom, have you been here all day? Have you seen anyone around?"

His mother paled. "What is it, Matt? What are you thinking?"

"The photos. They aren't in my room—anywhere." He looked at Sara. "Are you thinking what I am?"

Sara took a deep breath. "Probably," she said hesitantly.

"What are you two talking about?" Mrs. Roberts demanded.

"We think someone has broken in here and taken the photos." Matt spread his hands wide. "I'm sure they were right here—on this table—just last night."

A thoughtful look deepened in Mrs. Roberts' earnest gray eyes. "I left for a while," she said. "But not for more than half an hour."

"I'm going outside," Matt said. "I want to see if there's evidence of anyone coming through a window."

His mother shook her head. "I didn't lock the door when I left. If anyone came, they could have walked right in." She tilted her head. "Funny, I didn't notice it then, but Freda—she's my pet parakeet, Sara—Freda was chattering and horribly upset when I got back. I wonder . . ."

"If only birds could talk," Matt mused.

"But they can't," Sara said practically. "I think we should call Officer Peterson. He'll know what to do."

"Right. Besides, he has a copy of those prints, too. Remember?"

Sara nodded.

Mrs. Roberts led her to a small birdcage in her bedroom while Matt went to the telephone. Freda hopped back and forth on her perch, her green-and-gold feathers fluffed into an agitated ball.

"She's still upset," Mrs. Roberts said.

"Pretty bird. Pretty bird," Freda squawked, her beady eyes sparkling.

"Why, she does talk!" Sara exclaimed.

Mrs. Roberts laughed. "But of course!"

"Pretty bird. Pretty bird. Dave's gone. Dave's gone."

"And who is Dave, you nonsensical bird?" Sara rested her hand against the wire cage. Freda pecked at her fingers. "Ouch!" Sara cried. "You naughty bird!"

"Freda, be kind to our guest," Mrs. Roberts rebuked the parakeet. "Sara, you come into the kitchen when you're finished visiting," she said, turning to the door.

Sara nodded. "Talk, Freda," she commanded. "Tell me who Dave is."

But this time Freda merely looked indignant. She hopped into the far corner, ruffled her feathers and refused to even look at Sara.

"Silly bird," Sara murmured. But no amount of persuasion could induce Freda to turn around.

Sara joined Matt and his mom in the kitchen just as he related his phone conversation with Officer Peterson. "He thinks we're onto something big!" Matt exclaimed. "Of course, he didn't say that, but I could tell."

Opening the refrigerator, he took out a carton of milk, poured two glasses, and motioned for her to join them at the table. "Officer Peterson wants to talk to you, Sara," he said. "You're to call him as soon as you get home."

Sara shivered. Somehow she felt she'd rather leave the dark woods behind her. The memory of those grasping arms, the handkerchief tightening around her mouth . . .

She reached for the glass of milk, then set it down abruptly. "I'd rather not," she blurted. Her eyes met Matt's. She took a quick breath inward. There was something in his glance—a tenderness, a gentleness . . .

She looked down at the tablecloth in sudden confusion, not knowing what to say.

Matt reached across the table and touched her hand. "Instead of my taking you home, would you rather we made a quick trip across town to see a certain old house?"

Sara looked up quickly. His flashing smile reassured her, pushed back the dark forest with its tentacled shadows. Her own hand turned over and clasped his.

"Please," she said. "I'd like that."

15

The monotony of the freeway and the drone of traffic lured Sara into daydreams. Memories of the fluttering owl, the towering T-shaped nose of the tow vehicle, its pulley dangling like a broken arm, made her shiver.

"Are you all right, Sara?" Matt asked. "Maybe I should take you home."

Sara pulled her thoughts away from the dark woods. "No," she said. "The old house will help me forget. Besides, I can't help but feel it'll bring us one step closer to proof." Her voice lowered. "We have to discover something that will tie everything together. I hope I can find it in the dark."

"We'll find it," Matt assured her. "I looked at a map. Sara . . ."

She looked at him expectantly in the darkness, but he lapsed into a troubled silence. Sara could feel the unrest nibbling at his spirit. *It's beginning to affect me, too,* she thought. *Can it be that he's afraid of something I don't understand? That he doesn't really want to find out who's behind this crazy three-ring circus?*

She pushed her thoughts aside and concentrated instead on freeway exit numbers. They easily found the old house. It brooded alone behind the streetlights, its tall, narrow windows dark in the night.

"I don't think anyone's home," Sara said nervously.

Matt peered through the windshield. "I think I see a light in back."

He got out slowly. "Coming, Sara?"

She pushed hard on the handle and joined him on the sidewalk. "I hope Mrs. Schaffer isn't in bed."

"It's not that late, " Matt assured her.

"But for an older lady—"

Matt took her arm gently. "Would you rather go home?" he asked.

Sara shook her head. "No," she said. "I want very much to meet Brad's Aunt Edna. And I'd like a closer look at that vase, too."

Slowly, they walked down the narrow sidewalk. Sara remembered an edging of cheery yellow marigolds, but in the darkness it looked more like the outlines of a slithering snake.

"The light is coming from the kitchen," Sara observed in a low voice.

They stepped onto the porch and knocked. Soon the soft pad of footsteps was followed by the fluttering of a curtain. "Brad?" a voice questioned.

"N-no," Sara stammered. "I'm Sara, Brad's friend—"

The door opened. An elderly woman with thin gray hair curling around her face peered at them. Sara noticed her big, capable hands, the thrust of her long jaw.

"I'm looking for Brad."

The woman's steady, colorless eyes examined Sara quietly. "You're too pretty a girl to come looking for my Brad. No, not too pretty. Too sweet."

Matt stepped close behind Sara. "Sara knew him from the drive-through where she worked," he explained. "She hadn't seen him for a long time, and she was worried."

"Over my Brad?" Disbelief echoed in the old woman's voice.

Sara studied her closely, noting a look of patient endurance that enveloped her like a cloak.

"We . . . I knew him rather well," she explained. "And

then—all of a sudden he was gone. I was wondering if he was all right. . . ." Her voice died into an uncertain silence. She didn't know what else to say.

The old woman seemed to understand. She stepped aside, motioning them to enter."You'll have to excuse my surprise," she explained. "It's just that no one ever comes here asking about Brad. He's my nephew, you see. And he's always had such a time making friends—except for Dave and Roy. They come sometimes—and Brad's other uncle."

Her keen eyes examined Matt with open curiosity. "You aren't much like the others who have been here—except for Dave."

"Dave?" Matt asked. He leaned forward, a look of concern clouding his usually fine features. "Dave who?"

Brad's aunt only shook her head sadly. "I don't remember last names very well. But it's funny, you two do have a look about you. Same coloring, except his hair's lighter, but the general resemblance is there. Now about my Brad. You say you were worried?"

Sara licked her lips nervously. "He'd often come to the place I used to work. Then he asked me to meet him and . . . and . . ."

"He didn't show up."

"Right. Something happened that night, and I thought—"

"There was a hit-and-run accident," Matt explained. "Sara was concerned that Brad might have been involved—since she never saw him again."

The old woman nodded. "I see," she said, "I see. But, I hope he's not in trouble Miss . . . Miss . . ."

"My name is Sara Faulkner. And this is Matt."

"Sara. It's a good name. You can call me Aunt Edna, both of you. And about Brad, he's all I have left," her voice dwindled. "I sure hope he hasn't done anything wrong."

Pity for the old woman grew within Sara's heart. "I'm

sure he loves you," she stammered.

There was an answering gleam in Aunt Edna's eyes. "Oh yes!" she exclaimed. "I know he does. And sometimes he shows it, too. Not in big ways, but little ways. Like the vase . . ."

An unexplainable feeling burned in Sara's throat and squeezed it like a vise. She shot Matt an agonized glance, but he didn't see. All his attention focused on Aunt Edna.

"A vase?" he asked. "Did he give it to you as a gift?"

"Let me show it to you," Aunt Edna said. "It's really very old, I think. The cut glass has a purple haze that indicates an antique."

She stepped back from the alcove and disappeared into the gloomy living room.

"Matt," Sara whispered, "you shouldn't have—"

His look of utter incredulity stopped her. "I thought you wanted a closer look."

"I did then, but now . . . that poor old woman!"

She stopped abruptly as Aunt Edna came through the door, proudly clutching a cut-glass vase in her hand. "My mother had one of these years ago. But it was broken. Brad must have remembered."

Sara took the vase with trembling fingers. "It's beautiful," she breathed. "I'm so glad you showed it to us." She extended it to Matt, a pleading look in her gray eyes.

His fingers touched the glass lightly. "I bet it's beautiful when the sun shines through it," he said gently.

"It is," Aunt Edna assured him. "Several days ago I filled it with roses from my garden. They were white with a slight pink tint, and somehow the violet hue—" She took a deep breath, clearing her throat self-consciously. "To think my Brad—"

"I . . . I . . ." Sara stammered, "I think we'd better go now, Aunt Edna." She returned the vase to the old woman, patting her big, weather-beaten hand impulsively.

The old woman grasped Sara's hand and squeezed it warmly. "You're a nice girl, Sara. I appreciate your caring enough about Brad to come." A sudden shadowed look veiled her colorless eyes. "But, honey," she whispered, drawing her away from Matt's questioning eyes, "you stay away from my Brad. He's special to me because he's all I have. But dearie," she said, nodding toward the door, "he don't hold a candle to that boy back there."

A sudden warmth colored Sara's cheeks. "Could I come back?" she asked. "Not—not to see Brad—but to see you?"

The old woman's chin raised with dignity. The colorless eyes shone with character and refinement.

She's known better days, Sara thought with unexpected understanding. *But life has been hard for her. I wonder if I could be her friend.*

Aunt Edna nodded as though reading her thoughts. "You could come for breakfast some morning," she said. "I always eat about nine. And I get lonely."

They joined Matt in the alcove. Aunt Edna still clutched her cherished vase. Matt opened the door. The woman stood still, smiling at them, her eyes peering at Sara. "You come again, Sara. You don't have to call. Just remember, breakfast is always at nine."

They left her standing there.

"Oh, Matt!" Sara cried, when they were alone in the car. "It was so sad. And that vase. It is my mother's. But I'll never be able to tell her."

"You're sure?"

Sara nodded. She leaned back stiffly and closed her eyes. "I think *I* have troubles—then I see someone whose life has obviously been one long disappointment after another."

She opened her eyes. "I wish I could think of something awful to do to Brad. But that would only hurt her more."

"Sara," Matt reminded her, "Brad's already in for a heap of trouble. First, the hit-and-run, then, breaking into our houses, and now that car-stealing operation."

"We can't prove it!" Sara cried.

"We will," Matt said grimly. "We will, whether we like it or not."

16

Matt's vow to prove Brad's involvement "whether we like it or not" tormented Sara.

No matter who gets hurt? Oh, that poor old woman.

Sara's thoughts boiled relentlessly. She edged her shoulders next to the door of the pickup and stared into the night. There were car lights coming, and streetlights and neon lights glared harshly.

Back in the clearing, there would be moonlight mingled with starlight—a gentle, caring light—except it would glisten on an ugly dangling pulley, glint off broken cars.

"Don't, Sara," Matt entreated, reaching across the open space between them.

Sara drew farther into her corner. "Please, Matt. I need to think this through"—her voice caught—"alone."

Matt withdrew his hand. He looked straight ahead, paying extra attention to his driving.

Now I've done it, Sara thought. *I've turned him away, and I didn't mean to.* She closed her eyes and leaned back into the seat. *Oh, Lord, help me sort out my tangled feelings. Help me see what you are trying to teach me.*

Gradually, her emotions quieted. In her mind she drew a picture: a tree, a branch, an apple. Across the apple she printed just one word: trust. She knew that trust involved giving Aunt Edna into God's hands, trusting Him to bring healing into her life.

She looked up, startled, as the pickup stopped in front

of her house. She turned to Matt. "I'm sorry. After everything you've done—for me to go on a 'we can't hurt the poor old woman' trip . . ."

Matt lowered his head, his hands stroking the steering wheel in troubled silence. "Sometimes we have to make decisions that are right but painful," he said at last, "instead of wrong and comfortable."

Sara watched his hands move restlessly around and around the steering wheel. "Matt, what's bothering you? Really bothering you? It isn't just Brad and those awful stripped cars, is it?"

Matt grasped the wheel tensely. He took a deep breath, and his chin sank to his chest. "No, Sara. It's . . . my brother, Dave." His voice lowered. "I never told you. I hate to tell you now."

Sara slid across the seat in one quick motion. Her hand reached out and touched his cheek.

Matt caught it, holding it tightly. "I think . . . my mother and I think . . . that he's the one who came into the house . . . took those pictures."

"But—" Sara protested.

"I know it sounds preposterous," Matt said. "But it's not as much as you'd think. Sara, I told you he lives in Portland, but what I didn't tell you is that he rents an upstairs room near where you live. That's where I was going the night I was hit. At first I didn't connect him to it, but now I do. He knows who hit me, Sara. I'm convinced."

"He's the blond I described, the one who watched our house that morning?"

"Yes. But I didn't realize—not at first."

"Is that why you sort of—you know—seemed almost reluctant to. . . ?"

Matt nodded. "Remember when we followed the yellow-and-black Plymouth? I recognized Brad that day as Dave's friend and began to wonder. I didn't want to think that my own brother knew who had struck me down and wasn't saying anything."

He sighed. "I feel much the same way you do about Brad's Aunt Edna." His hand knotted into a fist. "Oh, why do the innocent have to suffer with the guilty? Why is it that when people sin, they always hurt other people?"

A lump formed in Sara's throat. She remembered her strange benefactor in the woods and started to speak. She shut her mouth quickly. He'd said, "Please, don't tell Matt." She hadn't understood then, but she did now. He was Dave, Matt's brother. He didn't want Matt to know he'd been there.

"I think," Matt pursued, "that Dave is involved with Brad and this Hot and Sweet character. But of course I don't really *know*."

I do, Sara wanted to cry out. *But what if I'm mistaken? Couldn't it be a mere coincidence that he was there?* Her thoughts circled like a baying hound treeing its prey.

He's kind, she thought. *Couldn't he have been there trying to protect us both from his friends?* "It's getting late," she said. "I'd better go in. Dad and Mom went out, and Aunt Nina's alone with Mandy."

"I'll walk you to the door," Matt offered. He got out and opened the door for her, holding out his hand.

She took it quietly. Somehow, their relationship had deepened. Their few moments of sharing had drawn them closer. They didn't need words as they walked up the steps and across the porch.

Sara reached for the doorknob, but her hand froze in consternation. A scuffling sound came through the closed door. She raised frightened eyes to Matt, then pushed the door open. A sharp exclamation and a dull thud propelled her through the living room and into the kitchen. She reached for the light switch.

The sudden light dazzled her eyes. "Aunt Nina!" she cried.

Aunt Nina perched triumphantly on a kitchen chair, her cane hooked around the neck of a man sprawled on the floor.

"I hit him good!" she cried, "and now I've caught him!" She gasped as the man began to thrash violently. "You're going to have to help me!" she screamed.

Matt pushed past Sara and bent over the intruder. The man turned his head.

Sara recognized the beefy face, the flashing eyes. "I know you!" she cried. "You were there the night of the accident!"

The fat man's lips drew murderously thin. His lips twisted and he spat straight at her. Sara turned her head quickly.

Matt slammed his fist into the big man's jaw.

"Call the police!" Matt hissed.

Sara grabbed the cane. "Please, Aunt Nina," she gasped.

But Aunt Nina cried, "I've got him!" and landed on all fours in the middle of his paunchy stomach.

After that, it was easy for Matt to twist a dish towel around the groaning man's hands while Sara stood ready with the cane. Aunt Nina escaped to the next room and began to dial. Hearing her excited words, Sara caught Matt's eye and smiled ruefully.

"He's here in the kitchen, right now," Aunt Nina explained over the phone. "I caught him myself. Why, I heard him come into the dining room while I was in the kitchen.

"I'd just come down for a drink and I couldn't find the light switch. Anyway, it was dark—real dark. I heard this noise in the next room, so I climbed up on a chair and waited. When he came within reach, I hit him with my cane.

I put his neck right there in the crook of my cane and kept fighting him."

"I wish I could see their faces," Sara giggled. "Do you suppose they've ever had a more unusual report?"

Matt smiled, but there was a hurt behind it that made Sara wince. She went over to the sink and turned on the water, splashing its fresh, cleansing warmth over her cheeks. Even though the fat man had missed, she wanted to be sure that not even a trace lingered.

Officer Peterson and another policeman arrived quickly. Sara and Aunt Nina let them in, and Boris pushed his way in behind them.

In her excitement, Aunt Nina talked nonstop as Sara led the way into the kitchen.

Aunt Nina's captive was sitting up, his eyes smoldering. "I'm not the only one in on this mess," he said belligerently. "I'll give you names—for a price." His sweeping gaze rested on Aunt Nina. "And that old hag," he said. "I can sue her!"

Sara's eyes flew to Matt's face. She saw her own consternation mirrored there.

"Names won't be necessary," Officer Peterson said quietly, "not with price tags. And neither are threats."

Sara stepped back. "I'll be in the living room if you want to question me." She took Aunt Nina's arm. "We both will."

She turned and left the men alone, thankful to be away from the fat man's dark gaze, grateful for Boris's presence beside her. The couch's softness welcomed her.

Boris came close, resting his beautiful brown muzzle in her lap. His dark eyes adored her.

"Where were you when we needed you?" Sara chided. She laid her hand between his ears. "You have your own set of problems don't you, Boris? Just like I have mine."

She looked up at her aunt prowling restlessly from window, to piano, to the door. "Come join me, Aunt Nina," she invited.

But Aunt Nina couldn't stop her pacing. She thumped her cane against the carpet and turned anxious eyes kitchenward.

"I hope they get my side of the story," she grumbled, "not just his."

"They already have, Aunt Nina," Sara reassured.

Aunt Nina turned her hand over and studied it. "I didn't know I had that much strength. I didn't even think about it. I just did it."

She frowned. "It hurts now," she said as she flexed her fingers experimentally. "I hope his neck hurts worse."

"Did he say anything?" Sara asked. "Before you hit him, I mean."

Aunt Nina snorted disdainfully. "He didn't have a chance. From the moment I hit him with my cane, all he could think of was leaving the neighborhood. I hope he's learned his lesson."

But Sara's thoughts had taken wing. She knew she would have to tell Officer Peterson about her experience in the dark woods. She'd have to tell him about Matt's brother.

Her dread increased as she wondered about the ugly spitting man with Matt and the policeman. Why had that curious fat man of the accident scene come into their kitchen? What had he been trying to do?

Sara shivered and sank deeper into the couch's softness.

17

A dirty bandana swayed from a dark branch. A dog barked. The handkerchief changed into a broken spiked collar dangling from a swinging ivy vine.

An unexplained hope leaped in Sara. She reached for the vine only to have it elude her, swinging farther and farther away, yet ever closer. Just as her hand closed around the collar, it disappeared. The ivy wrapped its long tendrils around her, and she was falling. . . .

Sara jerked awake. Her blanket twisted uncomfortably around her body, and she was hot and sweaty.

She struggled loose from the confining blanket and straightened her legs. Somehow, the ceiling seemed too low, the night too dark. She got up and pushed her curtains aside. A faint breeze from the window touched her cheeks.

The dark, heavy feeling persisted. *It must have been the dream,* Sara decided. *That, or last evening's excitement.*

Matt had been so quiet. He'd left with only a faint nod in her direction.

Then Officer Peterson took her aside, and she told him everything—the stranger in the dark woods, Aunt Edna's Brad, and how she and Matt had been fitting the pieces together.

Officer Peterson said little. He merely nodded and wrote. He had left with his customary assurance, "We're watching out for you."

Sara sighed. The ivy below her glinted silver in the

moonlight. In her dream, it had come closer. . . .

She switched on the light and reached for her sketchbook. If she could capture the vine on paper, it wouldn't be so threatening.

The vine grew beneath her fingers into a fairylike work of art, weaving itself around the edges of her page. After a while, she turned off the light. She could sleep now.

She wakened with a thought. "I suffered on the cross so that you might know me." She lay very still and let the warmth of it creep around her heart. One hand stole out and picked up her Bible.

She turned onto her side, drawing up her knees. "Jesus said He was the Vine," she mused, "and I a branch. That means He wants to be close to me—my own special friend."

The vine chapter reached out to her. Once again the command to bear fruit filled her with yearning.

She stopped reading, and her thoughts whispered, *Lonnie, Doreen, the customers at the drive-through—someday I'll work there again, only it will be different. God's love will shine through me.*

She read on, "My command is this! Love each other as I have loved you. Greater love has no one than this, that he lay down his life for his friends. You are my friends if you do what I command."

Tears dampened her lashes as she underlined the verses carefully. Then she lay back, closing her eyes. *Love each other. Friends. Since Jesus is my friend, I can be a friend to others.*

When Sara slipped out of bed the next morning, she knew what she must do.

The scent of roses greeted Sara as she turned onto the path leading to Aunt Edna's door. Although it was almost nine o'clock, dew still lingered on the roses' red, gold, pink, and white upturned faces.

Sara lingered, delighting in their fragrance and colorful beauty, prolonging the moment until she would have to face her uncertainties. Aunt Edna spared her the agony of waiting.

The door opened, and Sara looked again into the rugged, haunted face of the old woman. The sunshine unpityingly accentuated deeply etched wrinkles in her weather-roughened face.

She held the door open wide, squinting in the morning light.

Sara held out her hand. "Good morning, Aunt Edna. I've taken you up on your breakfast invitation."

A smile broke across Aunt Edna's features. "Sara," she said, "my friend. Come in, come in."

Sara's fears evaporated at the old woman's obvious delight in seeing her. She smiled and followed her inside, looking around curiously.

The kitchen was a wealth of homey clutter, the counters and walls strewn with odds and ends. Sara's roving eye picked out a cookie jar in the shape of a huge baby chicken, a snowy white teapot, a needlepoint wall hanging filled with a colorful assortment of cards and notes. Sara suspected they each held a memory.

Aunt Edna stepped to the stove and opened the oven. "It's my favorite kind of pancake," she explained. "It spreads itself in my skillet without any attention while I go about as I please."

She drew the blackened fry pan from the oven while Sara sniffed in appreciation. "I have fruit to put inside, and presto—there's breakfast fit for a queen." Her big hands slid it onto an old blue willow platter.

She opened the refrigerator and took out a bowl of fresh peaches and blueberries mixed together with apple slices and frozen strawberries.

"It looks wonderful, Aunt Edna."

"It is. And so easy. Now all I do is pour my coffee." Her hands halted in midair. "But, tell me, child, what do you want to drink? I have—let's see . . ."

"Just a glass of ice water," Sara said quickly. "I can't think of anything that would go better."

"Or cost less," Aunt Edna said shrewdly. "I think we're going to like each other, child."

The hot, fruit-filled pancake disappeared rapidly as Sara and the old woman got acquainted. They laughed and chatted, and Sara soon forgot the reason for her visit. She even pushed aside the old woman's relationship to the man she and Matt suspected of several serious crimes.

"Aunt Edna . . ." Sara began. "I wonder—"

Suddenly, the door opened, and Sara felt an instant sinking sensation. It flooded through her, plunging her downward. But mingled with her fear came a whisper. *I am your friend. I will never leave you or forsake you.*

Her chin thrust upward. "Hello, Brad," she said quietly. "I'll bet you never expected to find me here."

Brad stared at her. The enticing look that had once turned her to formless butter was gone. His brown eyes glowered at her from a hostile face.

Aunt Edna set her coffee cup down. "I'm sorry, Brad. I'm afraid we've eaten everything up. If you had told me—"

"It's all right," Brad said evenly. "I was just looking for a cup of coffee."

Sara leaped to her feet. She grabbed a cup from the mug tree and filled it with steaming brew from the pot.

He took the cup without a word and slammed out of the room.

"He has no manners," Aunt Edna sighed. "I've tried to teach him, but by the time I got him it was too late." She shook her head.

"It's never too late," Sara said gently. "Aunt Edna, could you show me your roses? Tell me their names? I'll help you do the dishes later."

Aunt Edna leaped at the suggestion. "Let's," she agreed. "Dishes we always have, but mornings like this . . ." She picked up a pair of garden shears and guided Sara toward the backyard.

"I never dreamed!" Sara cried in awe. A flaming flower design dominated the green lawn. Its center was a circle of yellow roses, its petals of variegated colors: yellow, white, salmon, peach, and of course, red.

As they walked among the flower beds, Aunt Edna told Sara their names and something of their history. "It's my hobby," she explained. Brandishing her garden shears, she clipped as she talked. Dead blossoms fell silently to the ground.

"I grew roses when my own children were growing up," she said, "and now Brad encourages me to do the same."

A lump came up in Sara's throat. *He can't be all bad if he likes Aunt Edna's roses.* "Your children," she said, "tell me about them."

Aunt Edna smiled sadly. "They're both gone. My son was killed in Vietnam, my daughter in a car accident not long afterward." She reached out and patted Sara's shoulder. "Don't look so sad, child. It happened long ago."

"And your husband?"

"Gone—when the children were still in school." She gestured toward the porch. "I've been cutting back that overgrown wisteria vine," she said. "It made me feel bad. Like my family, those branches are cut away—gone—forever."

Sara turned. The vine clinging to the porch had obviously covered much of it before beginning its ascent into the tall maple tree. But now many of its branches hung limply.

They walked over to it. Aunt Edna reached up and

pulled a withered branch forward. “See?” she said. “Cut off—dead.”

She dropped the withered branch onto the ground and pulled a leafy one forward. “This is my Brad,” she explained, “the only one I have left.” Her colorless eyes sharpened. “And now, Sara,” she said softly, “I think you’ve been trying to tell me something, something I don’t want to hear . . . about my Brad.”

18

Sara stood alone in the rose garden. It was behind her now, their suspicions expressed. But her devastating words had been coupled with a quiet assurance. As she looked at the withered vine on Aunt Edna's porch she'd recalled John 15. Somehow, she wanted to communicate what she had learned.

"You don't have to be alone," she had explained to the stricken woman. "When a person has Jesus Christ, that person has life." She had pulled her sketchbook from her purse and opened to the ivy vine.

Aunt Edna's trembling finger had touched the leaves gently as Sara explained about the vine and the branches, about Jesus Christ and His followers. When Aunt Edna had turned back toward the house, Sara ripped the page from its place and pressed it into her new friend's careworn hand.

Now Sara covered her face with her hands. Matt's words hammered inside her. "Sometimes we have to choose what is right but painful, instead of wrong and comfortable."

She shivered and looked up as a sudden shadow chilled her arms and shoulders. Brad stood between her and the sunshine, his arms folded menacingly.

"What did you tell her?" he demanded. "Why?"

Sara raised her chin. "Why?" she repeated. "Because the police will be here soon, asking questions. I know it all—the car stripping, the hit-and-run accident."

She took a step toward him, holding out her hand in a pleading gesture. "Why don't you give yourself up, Brad? You'd have a chance then. And Aunt Edna—"

Sara gasped as an unseen arm grabbed her brutally and thrust her hard against a maple tree. Someone's arm circled her waist while a hand clasped roughly over her mouth.

"You thought you could have it all your way!" Sara recognized Hot and Sweet's low voice. "Maybe you have another think coming."

Frantically, Sara twisted against his arm. But his strength was too much for her. She went limp.

A dim mist clouded her brain, distant voices intensifying her confusion. She struggled desperately, whispering, "Lord, please help . . ."

Slowly, the terrifying mist cleared. She lay on a lawn chair surrounded by faces that strangely faded in and out. Everything seemed unreal.

"Matt," she whispered.

"I'm right here," Matt assured her, "and so is Officer Peterson."

Another face, looking oddly like Matt's, swam into view. Only this face was long and thin. Confusion engulfed her, and she closed her eyes. Voices—there were too many voices—explaining, droning, going on and on.

The voices receded. When Sara opened her eyes again, she and Matt were alone. The leaves overhead whispered softly, and something moved close to her.

"Sara," Matt's voice said, "are you all right?"

"Yes," she answered.

Matt's hand touched her cheek lightly. "Take your time getting up, Sara. There's no rush."

But there was. Brad, Hot and Sweet, Matt's brother, and Officer Peterson had all been there while she. . . . She sat up. She was still under Aunt Edna's big maple tree, surrounded by roses. Beside her, withered wisteria branches littered the yard. Matt knelt beside her, a worried frown squinting his eyes.

"Matt," she cried, "what happened?"

Matt reached for her hand. He held it while he detailed his and Officer Peterson's arrival and the subsequent arrest.

"We caught Hot and Sweet attacking you, Sara. Brad just stood there. It was terrible."

Sara shuddered. "Poor Aunt Edna," she whispered.

"She's all right, Sara. In a way I think it was a relief to her. Sometimes knowing is better than guessing."

"Matt, your brother. I saw him here. I know I did."

"Yes, Dave was here. But in that case, I guessed wrong. And I couldn't be more thankful."

The hand clasping hers trembled slightly. "He wasn't involved with Brad or Hot and Sweet, at least not in the way I thought. He was sleuthing them out on his own, even though they were his friends." His voice lowered, "Because of me and you."

"I know," Sara said. "Remember when I was tied to the tree in the woods? Dave came to me and cut me loose."

"But I thought you'd—"

"No. Hot and Sweet—or was it Brad?—tied me too tightly. I couldn't get away. I didn't tell you because Dave asked me not to. Besides, I didn't *really know* he was your brother—not then."

Her forehead wrinkled as she tried to concentrate. "I'm still mixed up. I can't put it all together yet. Could you go back over it? Try to explain?"

Matt took a deep breath. "It all began the night a friend of mine told me Dave had a room close to where you live. I think I told you that. But what I didn't know until today was that Brad's uncle was his roommate—and Aunt Nina's intruder."

Sara gasped. Matt squeezed her hand tighter. "Brad stumbled into Dave's room the night of my accident, yelling that he'd killed or injured someone. Brad's uncle went into action, found out it was only a few blocks away, and rushed out, saying he'd take care of everything."

Sara shuddered. "The way he grabbed my arm—"

"I know. While all that was happening, Brad explained to Dave that he had been driving a car with a faulty title, and that when he had the accident, he panicked.

"Brad paced around and around the room, finally asking Dave to go back the next morning and see if he could find the camera that had fallen out of the car."

"Did Dave know that the photos inside were evidence?"

"No. At that point he knew nothing about what was going on in the clearing. Brad had even told him that the car he was driving belonged to a friend!

"Later that day, Dave called the hospital and asked questions. A helpful nurse identified the victim of the hit-and-run accident. That was when he determined to do everything he could to unravel exactly what Brad was doing. He'd thought that something suspicious was going on before, but he didn't know what."

"And the roommate? Brad's uncle? Did he suspect him?"

"Yes. Actually Brad's uncle was the instigator of the whole operation. He started out small and became a quick success. He dragged Brad into—"

"What about Hot and Sweet? Where does he fit?"

"He's Brad's friend. Brad asked him to keep an eye on you at the restaurant, because he knew you were the probable guardian of the camera. Brad talked Hot and Sweet into searching your house each time—"

"The collar!" Sara exclaimed. "The stereo!"

"And your grandmother's vase," said a gentle voice behind her.

Sara turned, withdrawing her hand from Matt's. She

started to take the vase that was extended to her, then shook her head.

"No, Aunt Edna. Not now. I want you to keep it for a while. I'll talk to my mother. She'll understand."

Aunt Edna smiled. "I don't really need it, child. But if it makes you feel better, and if it's all right with your parents, I'll hang on to it. It'll remind me of you and your promise to come again."

Sara rose to her feet and embraced her. "Oh, Aunt Edna. I'll come once a week. We'll talk and eat breakfast—"

The old woman nodded. "I'll look forward to it, then. You're a lovely girl. And I think a real friend."

She went back inside while Sara stared after her wistfully.

"I'm glad you've become friends with her, Sara. Don't worry. God will help us find answers."

Sara sighed heavily and sat back down. "I know He will. Now, where were we?"

"Let's go to the yellow-and-black Plymouth. I told you I recognized Brad as Dave's friend. I began to wonder if Dave was somehow connected with the break-ins at your house and the initial accident. It really hurt me—my own brother."

"And he was?"

"Yes, but not like I'd imagined. Dave told us he was the one who took the photos from our house. His roommate was getting ugly, telling him he'd better produce or his little brother and his girl would be hurt. Brad and Hot and Sweet were getting nasty, too.

"That was the reason Dave had been skulking around the clearing. He knew Brad's uncle, Brad, and Hot and Sweet had a junkyard where they fooled around. But he didn't know the extent of the operation until last night."

"And now we all know," Sara murmured. "Including the police. I'm glad—glad that it's being stopped."

"So am I. Something else, Sara. Before Brad left, I told him we'd look out for his Aunt Edna. I couldn't tell for sure, but I think he was touched.

"Dave went to the police station with them, too. He told me he wanted to help if he could. Somehow that made me breathe easier. And Sara, I'm happy about something else, too."

Sara looked at him quickly, then lowered her eyes. "What, Matt?"

"Us," he said simply.

"What made you—I mean, how come. . . ?"

Matt smiled. "Are you asking me what drew me to you, Sara? At first it was simply your name."

"My name? Matt, you'll have to do better than that!"

"I will! Let me explain. Several years ago, I noticed something in the life of Sarah in the Old Testament that changed my own life. Remember how argumentative she could be, and how mean she was to Hagar?"

Sara nodded. "Go on."

"I read something in Hebrews 11 that really threw me. Sarah—that mean, ruthless lady—was called a woman of faith! I went back to Genesis, determined to find out why."

"And did you?"

Matt nodded. "I saw how she laughed at God in unbelief when she learned she was going to give birth to a son in her old age. And then I found something else—in a name."

"Wow. You must have done some real research."

"I did. Her son Isaac's name means laughter. After Sarah laughed in unbelief, God changed her and transformed that laughter into believing laughter."

"That's right!" Sara exclaimed.

"See how God transformed her attitude? At her son's birth, she said that his name would be Isaac. And that everyone who saw him would laugh with her!"

"And her name is in the hall of faith in Hebrews 11," Sara marveled, "because she finally recognized that without God, she could do nothing—that she was totally dependent on Him for everything." Sara's fingers stole to her cross necklace. "Even changing her attitude."

"Yes," Matt agreed. "Sarah is a picture of God's grace . . . a princess of faith and laughter."

"A princess? Where do you get that?"

"From her name. Sarah means princess." He smiled at Sara and she knew he wasn't thinking of the Sarah in the Bible anymore. A flush rose in her cheeks as he drew her close to him.

She felt very special.